W9-ARX-796

"Is something bothering you, son?"

Lucas didn't really expect an answer. Still, he always conversed with Mark as if the tyke might actually speak.

"Want Felicity for my mother." Each word was pronounced separately, slurred but discernible.

Euphoria filled Lucas. "You spoke!" He lifted his son and gave him a huge hug.

The boy looked into his father's face. "Want Felicity for my mother," he repeated.

Still in a state of shock, Lucas wanted to make sure he understood. "You want me to marry Felicity Burrow?"

Mark nodded furiously.

A smile played at the corners of Lucas's mouth. "Seems we're on a similar wavelength. We've each found something we can't live without—and it's the same thing."

Thinking of sweet, stubborn Felicity, Lucas grinned. He'd start with flowers, he decided. "I'll see what I can do, son. I'll see what I can do...."

Dear Reader;

Silhouette Romance begins the New Year with six heartwarming stories of the enduring power of love. Felicity Burrow thought she would never trust her heart again—until she met Lucas Carver and his darling little boy in *A Father's Vow*, this month's FABULOUS FATHER by favorite author Elizabeth August.

Love comes when least expected in Carolyn Zane's *The Baby Factor*, another irresistible BUNDLES OF JOY. Elaine Lewis was happy to marry Brent Clark—temporarily, of course. It was the one way to keep her unborn baby. What she didn't bet on was falling in love!

Karen Rose Smith's emotional style endures in *Shane's Bride*. Nothing surprised Shane Walker more than when Hope Franklin walked back into his life with a little boy she claimed was his. Loving little Christopher was easy, but trusting Hope again would prove a lot harder. Could Hope manage to regain Shane's trust and, more important, his love?

The sparks fly fast and furiously in Charlotte Moore's *The Maverick Takes a Wife*. When Logan Spurwood fought to clear his name, Marilee Haggerty couldn't resist helping him in his search for the truth. Soon she yearned to help him find strength in her love, as well....

And two couples discover whirlwind romance in Natalie Patrick's *The Marriage Chase* and *His Secret Son* by debut author Betty Jane Sanders.

Happy Reading!

Anne Canadeo

Please address questions and book requests to:
Silhouette Reader Service
U.S.: 3010 Walden Ave., P.O. Box 1325, Buffalo, NY 14269
Canadian: P.O. Box 609, Fort Erie, Ont. L2A 5X3

ELIZABETH AUGUST

A FATHER'S VOW

Silhouette
ROMANCE™
Published by Silhouette Books
America's Publisher of Contemporary Romance

To Cottie and Myra...whose hearts are always open.

 SILHOUETTE BOOKS

ISBN 0-373-19126-X

A FATHER'S VOW

This edition published by arrangement with Harlequin Books S.A.

® and TM are trademarks of Harlequin Books S.A., used under license. Trademarks indicated with ® are registered in the United States Patent and Trademark Office, the Canadian Trade Marks Office and in other countries.

Printed in U.S.A.

ELIZABETH AUGUST

lives in western North Carolina, with her husband, Doug, and her three boys, Douglas, Benjamin and Matthew. She began writing romance novels soon after Matthew was born. She's always wanted to write.

Elizabeth does counted cross-stitching to keep from eating at night. It doesn't always work. "I love to bowl, but I'm not very good. I keep my team's handicap high. I like hiking in the Shenandoahs, as long as we start up the mountain so the return trip is down rather than vice versa." She loves to go to Cape Hatteras to watch the sun rise over the ocean.

Elizabeth August has also published books under the pseudonym Betsy Page.

Fabulous Fathers

Dear Mark,

Having you for my son is a unique and wonderful experience. One that I will always cherish.

I now realize that through me you have inherited an ability that will make your life in some ways more interesting and in some ways more difficult. I can only hope this talent will enrich your existence as it has mine.

It was this ability that drew us to Felicity. It made you realize that she is the mother you want and proved to me that she is the wife I have sought. Her mind and mine bond in a way that is uniquely ours. I hope that in time you will find someone with whom your mind will match, as well. I cannot describe the experience. It will startle you at first, but I guarantee it will add a dimension to your life you cannot imagine nor can words describe.

Your loving father,

Lucas

Chapter One

"Well, it seems that a Zebulon Lansky was alive at the time this was printed," Lucas Carver announced to his four-year-old son as he put aside the pencil-thin, magazine-size phone directory for Smytheshire, Massachusetts, and vicinity. Getting here had required a long flight and a drive over winding mountainous roads but finding a Lansky, especially one with the same name as the man he sought, was worth the trouble. "Of course, we can't know if this Zebulon Lansky is the one we're looking for. My guess is he's a son or grandson."

The boy, blue eyed and blond haired like his father, merely nodded solemnly, then ate another bite of his hamburger.

"Did you find what you were looking for?" the waitress asked in a friendly voice, approaching and pouring more coffee into Lucas's cup.

"Maybe. Thanks for the use of the directory," he replied, in an equally friendly tone. The café, situated on

Main Street, had a comfortable, homey atmosphere.
The food was of the healthy country variety with a limited but sufficient menu. It was well past the lunch hour
but before the dinner hour, thus he and his son were the
only customers other than two men drinking coffee at
a table a short distance away. Good timing, he mentally patted himself on the back. He hadn't wanted to
draw any attention to himself or his son. "I was wondering if you could tell me how to get to Hollow Road."

The waitress's brow furrowed in concentration.
"Hollow Road," she repeated, the furrows deepening.
"No, can't say as I can. It isn't in town. I can tell you
that." Turning to the other occupied table, she asked,
"Chief Brant, do you know where Hollow Road might
be?"

The brown-haired man who had been sitting with his
back to Lucas turned. The friendly greeting on his face
suddenly became guarded. Rising, he walked over to
Lucas's table.

Watching the tall, broad-shouldered man, who
looked to be in his mid-thirties, approach, Lucas realized he was wearing a uniform and recalled that the
waitress had addressed him as Chief Brant. So much for
trying to be inconspicuous, Lucas thought dryly. Looks
like the second person he was going to meet in town was
the chief of police.

He felt a prickling on his neck and glanced across the
table to see his son staring at him worriedly. He gave the
boy a wink to let him know everything was all right.
After all, they had nothing to hide. He'd merely wanted
to keep his business here private.

"I'm Thatcher Brant." The chief extended his hand
toward Lucas as he reached the table.

"Lucas Carver," he said, rising to accept the handshake. His six-foot-one-inch height and athletic build came close to matching the policeman's slightly larger frame. The lawman's grip was strong, he noted. This was a man who could take care of himself in a fight. But more important, Lucas sensed a strong honesty and decency in the lawman. Still, there was a guardedness about Chief Brant that made him uneasy. Lucas hadn't come here looking for trouble. Releasing the policeman's hand, he smiled and forced a friendly nonchalance into his voice. "And this is my son, Mark."

Thatcher's gaze shifted to the child. His features softened noticeably, and he extended his hand to the boy. "Pleased to meet you."

For a moment, Mark simply looked hard at the big man, then he smiled shyly and accepted the handshake. Thatcher grinned and the boy's smile broadened. As if satisfied that all was well, Mark returned to eating his hamburger.

"There's not much down Hollow Road except a few residences. Are you looking for someone in particular?" Thatcher asked.

His tone was friendly, but Lucas sensed a protectiveness behind the man's casual question. Small communities take care of their own, he reminded himself. Wanting the lawman to know he was not here to make trouble, Lucas said, "As a matter of fact, I am. Zebulon Lansky."

"Zebulon Lansky?" The waitress repeated with surprise.

Lucas noticed the elderly man who'd been sitting with the police chief suddenly straighten and take more interest. As for the chief, his guardedness increased.

The waitress frowned and shook her head. "Don't know why anyone'd go looking for that cantankerous old hermit."

Lucas sensed a rush of apprehension and glanced at his son to see the boy holding his hamburger poised in front of his mouth as he again stared worriedly at his father. Again, Lucas gave him a reassuring wink. But this time, Mark didn't relax. Instead he turned to look at the waitress, his anxiousness clearly evident in his expression.

"Don't worry, son. Zebulon wouldn't hurt anyone," Thatcher said.

Lucas turned to find the chief smiling comfortingly at Mark.

"Yeah," the waitress spoke up quickly. "I didn't mean to frighten you. It's just that hardly anyone ever goes looking for Zebulon. He doesn't exactly invite company."

Mark's gaze traveled around the trio, then came to rest on his father. After a moment, he returned to eating his hamburger.

The waitress went back to the counter. Lucas seated himself while Thatcher took out a pen and began drawing a map, giving instructions as he sketched out the route Lucas should take. "Zebulon's place is at the end of the road," the lawman finished.

"Thanks." Lucas slipped the napkin into his pocket.

Thatcher nodded and walked back to the table across the room. Still standing, he put money down to cover his bill. "Got to be getting back to work, Doc," he said, picking up the tan Stetson lying on one of the chairs. Giving the waitress a wave, he headed to the door.

Mark's gaze jerked to the elderly man. In the next instant, he was out of his chair and trying to climb into his father's lap.

"I didn't bring you here to see another doctor," Lucas assured the boy.

The tall, elderly man rose from his chair. "You don't have to be afraid of me, son," he said. "I'm retired. Reid Prescott's the doc now. I just cover for him once in a while." He also dropped some money on his table but instead of leaving, he approached Lucas and Mark and smiled with understanding. "I'm used to kids being a mite uncomfortable around doctors." His gaze narrowed as he studied the man holding the boy. "I once saw a picture of Zebulon in his younger years. Your face is the mirror image of the one in the photograph, and you've got the Lansky blue eyes."

"How old is the Zebulon Lansky we're talking about?" Lucas asked, making certain to keep his voice casual.

"He told me he was born the same year this town was founded. That'd make him ninety-six by my reckoning."

Lucas had to fight to keep his expression nonchalant. He couldn't believe his good fortune. The man he had come here hoping to learn about was still alive.

"I wish I could be there when he sees the two of you," Doc mused with a twinkle in his eyes. "Should be real interesting." He gave them a friendly smile. "Keep in mind that his bark's worse than his bite."

Maybe "good fortune" wasn't exactly the right description after all, Lucas thought watching the elderly man depart. Considering the waitress's reaction to the mention of Zebulon's name and the retired doctor's caution, he was beginning to think that the meeting he was planning could be an even more difficult encounter than he'd anticipated.

Mark had slipped off his lap and was again eating his lunch. Lucas looked protectively at the boy. He had no choice. For his son's sake, he had to speak to Zebulon Lansky.

Felicity Burrow stopped hoeing and looked skyward. The late-afternoon sky had been clear when she'd come out to do a little weeding in the vegetable garden beside the house she shared with her grandmother. But the feeling that a storm was brewing had been growing stronger with each passing moment.

Her gaze scanned directly above the garden then traveled along the tops of the mountains surrounding the valley. Only a few white fluffy clouds floated lazily in the heavens. "I could have sworn something was coming our way," she muttered under her breath, peering harder toward the mountain as if expecting a huge thunderhead to suddenly come rolling into view.

Her grandmother stepped out onto the front porch, waved, then sat down in one of the rocking chairs and began piecing together a square for the new quilt she'd just begun.

Felicity waved back. Usually the sight of the white-haired, seventy-two-year-old woman in her loose fitting housedress and comfortable shoes, sitting sewing was soothing. In fact, Felicity couldn't think of a time when her grandmother's presence hadn't helped ease her mind. Even when her parents had died tragically, leaving her orphaned at the age of eighteen, her grandmother had been able to help her past a pain she thought she could not endure. And since her grandfather's death, she felt even closer to the short, slightly

plump woman on the porch. But today her grandmother couldn't lessen the feeling that something was
stirring in the air. The muscles across the top of her
back tightened until they were painful. Again hoping
physical exercise would help, she returned to her hoeing.

A hoed row of corn later, she had to admit that the
physical activity wasn't helping. A nagging sense of
anticipation, as if something important was about to
happen, continued to grow. Abruptly she strode to the
porch. But rather than mounting the step, she stood
beside it, leaning against the railing and again looking
toward the mountains. "I could swear a storm is brewing," she announced with a perplexed frown.

Thelma Burrow leaned a little forward to get a fuller
view from beneath the porch roof. "Sky looks clear to
me."

Felicity's frown deepened. "I know." Taking off her
wide-brimmed straw hat, she wiped the perspiration
from her brow on the sleeve of her shirt, then briskly
ruffled her short auburn hair. The sweat-soaked tresses
sent out a light spray of water. She could feel the natural curl already taking command.

"Your instincts aren't normally so far off the mark."
Brown eyes that matched her granddaughter's studied
Felicity from a face wrinkled by weather and age. "Did
something happen at the office today to upset you?"

Felicity shook her head. "Nothing. It was a boring
day. That's why I came home early." She raked a hand
through her hair, combing uselessly at the tangling mass
of drying curls. "Truth is, I've been restless all day."

Thelma smiled knowingly. "You always hoe when
something's bothering you."

"But I usually know what's nagging at me. Today I haven't got a clue. I just keep feeling as if something is going to happen. It's like there's an added electricity in the air."

Concern spread over the older woman's features as she peered more closely at her granddaughter. "Are you expecting whatever is going to happen to be bad?"

Felicity thought hard for a moment. "No, not bad. At least I don't think so." An incredibly strong wave of expectation suddenly swept through her, and she jerked her gaze to the road.

"There's a car coming," Thelma announced, setting aside the patch she'd been working on in preparation for greeting visitors.

But the car, a green, two-door coupe, didn't pull into their driveway. Instead it continued down the road.

"Is that Colin and Madaline Darnell?" Thelma asked, squinting at the passing vehicle for a better focus. "I'll admit these old eyes aren't as good as they used to be but that didn't look like them to me."

"No. It was a man and young boy. I couldn't see the man very well but the boy was blond with blue eyes. A cute kid." Felicity was amazed by how clear her image of the child was. The road was a good two hundred feet from the house and the car had passed quickly, but she recalled the young blond-haired, blue-eyed boy looking out the window as if he'd been right in front of her. "They weren't locals. I won't swear to knowing all of our fifteen hundred residents on a first-name basis, but I'm fairly certain I know them all by sight. And, we'd have heard if there were any newcomers moving in."

"I spoke to Zebulon today. He's not expecting any visitors and nobody'd bother him unannounced. They must be on their way to visit the Darnell's," Thelma speculated. Abruptly she frowned. "I didn't know Colin and Madaline were back."

"They aren't," Felicity replied. "Madaline's baby is due soon, and she told me they're staying at their home in Boston until after the birth. Besides, both of them are so busy with their careers they never get out to their place here except on rare weekends and this is a weekday."

Thelma frowned in the direction the car had gone. "Then whoever was in that car must be lost."

Felicity nodded. "That'd be my guess."

Thelma's frown deepened. "I hope old Zebulon and that dog of his don't give them a fright."

Felicity frowned, too, as she continued to stare in the direction in which the green coupe had gone. Beyond their place was the Darnells' land, then Zebulon's holding. The road ended at the old man's gate.

"Of course they could be friends of the Darnells, and Colin and Madaline are letting them use their place," Thelma continued to speculate.

"Maybe," Felicity conceded, her restlessness stronger than ever. "I'm going to hoe some more," she announced abruptly and headed back to the garden.

The car, she noted after ten minutes, had not returned down the road. Whatever the man and boy had been seeking, they must have found it. Wishing the restlessness that continued to plague her would subside, she hoed more vigorously.

As he parked in his driveway and climbed out of the car, Thatcher Brant waved to his six-year-old daughter and nine-year-old son playing in the backyard. Going inside, he lifted Joseph, the newest addition to the Brant clan, out of the playpen in the kitchen. The child giggled with delight. Cradling the baby in his arm, he strode to the sink where his wife was snapping beans for dinner and slipped his free arm around her waist.

Samantha Brant glanced up at her husband to accept his kiss with a welcoming smile. Almost immediately her expression turned to one of concern. "What's wrong?" she asked.

"The blond-haired man and boy showed up today."

"The ones I saw in the crystal?"

He nodded. "The man is Lucas Carver and the boy is his son, Mark."

"Do you think they're trouble?"

"They're looking for Zebulon Lansky. It's my guess they're more likely to *find* trouble than to make any."

"My grandpa used to say that Zebulon was merely a private person, not really a difficult one."

"He's never gone out of his way to cause any trouble," Thatcher conceded. "But he does guard his privacy zealously."

"If you're worried, you have time to take a quick drive out there before dinner," Samantha suggested.

Thatcher nodded. "I think I will, just to make sure Mr. Carver didn't get lost."

Samantha laid a restraining hand on her husband's arm. "When I was dusting today, I happened to look into the crystal again. The man and boy were there and so was Felicity Burrow."

Thatcher frowned. "Maybe Mr. Carver has some legal business he needs to discuss with Zebulon."

"Maybe," Samantha agreed.

Chapter Two

Lucas braked to a halt. Hollow Road had ended abruptly. Woods were all that was in front of him and to either side except for a single-lane gravel road. A mailbox with the name Lansky painted on it stood on a post beside the road. About ten feet farther was a gate with a prominently displayed sign stating that this was Private Property.

Lucas gave Mark an encouraging grin. "This must be the place."

Mark nodded, his expression one of uncertainty.

Pulling onto the gravel roadway, Lucas again wondered what would be the best way to approach Zebulon Lansky. With caution, he decided, as he stopped to open the gate, drove through, then stopped to close the gate. Of course he'd always planned to proceed with caution. There were other lives to consider.

Beyond the gate, the narrow road wound through densely forested land. About the time Lucas was beginning to wonder if there was actually a house at the end of this driveway, he entered a large clearing. Situated near the center stood a single-story rambling structure that looked as if it had started as a one-room cabin then been built onto as need or fancy dictated. An old man was sitting in a rocking chair on the porch whittling, his face mostly obscured by a thick mustache and long white beard. A full head of snowy hair hung to his shoulders and beyond. He was wearing a red plaid shirt, worn jeans and high hunting boots. On the wall behind him but near enough at hand to be easily accessible was a rifle. A medium-size, brown-and-black, long-haired dog lay close by.

Lucas parked. As he started to get out of the car, the dog was on its feet instantly. Its relaxed manner gone, it snarled then began barking furiously. A small hand gripped Lucas's arm warningly. He turned to see fear in his son's eyes. Maybe the boy was right, he decided as the dog left the porch and came to stand about four feet from his door, its teeth bared in preparation to defend its master.

Lucas closed the door and rolled down his window. "I'm looking for Zebulon Lansky," he called out.

The old man eased out of his chair and moved toward the porch rail for a better view of his visitors. "Who's looking?"

"My name's Lucas Carver and this is my son, Mark." Lucas wondered if coming here had been wise. This aged woodsman was very different from the dapper figure cut by Andre Molieau, his great-grandmother's long since deceased husband. The small hand gripping his arm gripped harder. He glanced at his son and his hesitation vanished. He would face the gates of Hell to help the boy.

"You found him," the old man called back.

The dog started barking again.

"Mutt, shut up and go lay down," Zebulon ordered. Picking up the rifle, he cradled it as he stepped off the porch.

The dog gave Lucas a final warning glance then, moving into the shade of the nearby ancient oak, he lay down. Still, he kept his eyes on the car and its occupants.

Zebulon's expression changed to one of surprise as he drew near his visitors. "You're a Lansky. Seen that same face peering at me out of my mirror sixty or so years ago." Blue eyes that matched Lucas's and his son's scrutinized them with interest. "The boy's a Lansky, too."

"Yes," Lucas admitted, the worry about how this confession might affect his grandmother, causing a renewed flare of anxiousness.

Zebulon suddenly stepped back and raised the rifle at the ready. "You can't be a Lansky. My great-grandfather was the only offspring of an only son. So was my grandfather, my father and myself. I'm the last of the Lansky bloodline." The interest in his eyes turned to cold accusation. "This is a trick to get your hands on my land. Well, whoever you are and whoever put you up to this had better understand that I've still got a few good years left in me."

Staring down the barrel of the gun, Lucas again doubted his wisdom in coming here. A hand tightening on his arm reminded him of his purpose. "I've got no interest in your land or anything you own. I've come looking for information. That's all."

Zebulon continued to regard him with suspicion. "What kind of information?"

Lucas met the old man's gaze steadily. "My son has never spoken. I've had every available test performed on him, and the doctors and therapists tell me there is nothing physically wrong with him. He's bright. He understands what's being said to him. He simply refuses to communicate verbally."

"T'ain't no history of muteness in the Lansky clan," Zebulon growled.

"He's not mute. He cries, and he laughs. He makes sounds. He simply won't talk."

"Maybe he just don't have nothing he thinks is worth saying."

Lucas frowned grimly. He'd hoped for an answer and a way to help his son. Clearly there wasn't one here. "Sorry I've wasted your time."

Turning to Mark, he eased his son back into his seat. "Looks like we were on a wild-goose chase after all," he said apologetically, while he refastened the seat belt around the boy. Expecting his son to show relief that they were leaving, instead he sensed regret and saw the boy look again at the old man and then at the dog as if he was sorry to be parting company.

"I suppose they are an interesting pair," he admitted ruffling the boy's hair. "But they can't help us, and they sure don't want us here."

As he turned the car and started back down the long driveway, he saw Zebulon in his rearview mirror. The old man was still standing where he'd left him. It was impossible to read an expression on the bearded face, but suddenly Lucas was certain there was something the aged woodsman had not told him. "Maybe we'll stick around a little longer."

Mark nodded to let his father know he liked this idea.

* * *

Felicity was working her way along a row of potato plants when she heard a car. Glancing toward the road, she saw the green coupe. A sense of frustration so strong it caused her hands to tighten around the handle of the hoe swept through her. She knew without a doubt the sensation had come from the occupants or an occupant in the car. Concluding that she and her grandmother had guessed rightly about the driver being lost, she watched the vehicle disappearing in the distance.

Abruptly she frowned in puzzlement. She was used to sensing emotions in other people, but never this strongly and certainly not from such a distance. "For some reason, my intuition is definitely working overtime," she muttered to herself.

Again she gazed skyward. Maybe one of those summer electrical storms was brewing just beyond the mountains. Through the years, she'd noticed that whenever there was a lot of lightning flashing, her instincts seemed to function more sharply.

A few minutes later she was putting away the hoe when she heard another car and saw Thatcher Brant drive by. There was certainly a lot of activity on their quiet little road today, she mused. A worried frown suddenly creased her brow. Maybe she should give Zebulon a call. She shook her head at this thought. If he needed her, he'd call her.

Still, she kept an eye out until she saw Thatcher's car returning down the road. As he passed, he waved a friendly greeting and she waved back. Obviously there wasn't anything amiss down Zebulon's way. "By midnight we'll probably be in the midst of the worst thunderstorm we've had in years," she declared, certain it was the weather that had her instincts so on edge.

"Something is obviously bothering you mightily," her grandmother remarked as Felicity entered the house to wash up for dinner.

Felicity shrugged. "I'm sure it's just a storm coming," she replied, but her words sounded hollow to her as if they lacked the ring of truth.

Thelma continued to study her with concern. "Must be some storm."

Felicity hadn't meant to worry her grandmother. She forced a grin and gave the elderly woman a hug. "We'll weather it."

A feistiness glistened in the old woman's eyes. "Of course we will."

A couple of hours later, Felicity was drying the last of the dinner dishes when the phone rang.

"That was a short conversation," Thelma observed when Felicity hung up after barely a minute.

"It was Zebulon. He wants me to pick him up and take him into town. He says he has to meet with someone, and he wants me there as his lawyer." Felicity frowned down at her jeans. They were the same ones she'd been hoeing in. "He wants me to come immediately, just as I am."

"Then I'd suggest you go," Thelma said.

"At least I put on a clean shirt when I came in to wash up for dinner," Felicity muttered to herself as she slipped on her sneakers, grabbed her purse off the hall table and strode out the front door.

Climbing into her car, she wondered who Zebulon wanted to see so urgently. The image of the little boy in the green coupe suddenly filled her mind. Behind him was the shadowy profile of the driver. Could they be responsible for her client's call? The restlessness she'd been feeling all day intensified. Shake it off! she ordered herself. Zebulon had requested his lawyer and she needed to be clearheaded.

Pushing the image of the man and boy from her mind, she glanced at herself in the rearview mirror. She'd brushed her sweat-soaked hair into reasonable order when she'd come in for dinner. To her relief, it had dried into an acceptable style, a bit too curly for her taste, but acceptable. Her face was another matter. Before going out to hoe, she'd washed off her makeup and without it she looked much younger than her twenty-eight years. That could be a disadvantage if Zebulon needed her to throw some legal weight around. Quickly she applied a touch of lipstick when she stopped to open the gate blocking his driveway.

Pulling up in front of his house, she found Zebulon waiting on the porch. He nodded his approval at her quick response to his request. "We're going to Betty Truesdale's place," he informed her, climbing into the passenger seat. Then he fell silent.

Felicity again thought of the man and the boy. Betty Truesdale was the owner of the Apple Tree Inn, a quaint, comfortable bed and breakfast on Apple Street and one of the few places in Smytheshire a stranger could find a room for the night. "I might be of more help if you'd tell me what this is all about," she coaxed, driving back to the main road.

"In this instance, you'll be of more help to me if you don't know anything in advance," the old man replied. "I trust your instincts, and I don't want them clouded by any preconceived notions."

Felicity glanced at her passenger. When her great-grandfather had come to Smytheshire and began his law practice, the Lanskys had been among his first clients. They'd remained clients when her grandfather had

eventually taken over the firm. And, she'd had no
doubt that had her father lived, they would have remained his clients as well. But her father had not lived
and when her grandfather had died two years ago, and
she'd become the sole lawyer in the practice, she'd been
certain Zebulon would seek other legal counsel. She'd
been fresh out of law school with little experience. But
Zebulon had stayed when others she'd considered
friends and supporters had chosen to go elsewhere.

Now she realized why. She'd sensed a certainty in
Zebulon when he'd mentioned her instincts. She did not
know how, but she was sure he'd guessed that she could
tell if a person was lying or not. This ability had helped
her a great deal in choosing and dealing with clients.

Of course, it was not always entirely accurate. People, she knew, lied for other reasons than being guilty
of misconduct. But her instincts had improved with age
and experience.

As they entered town and turned down Apple Street,
she sensed a heightened electricity in the air. It was unnerving and yet invigorating at the same time. Pulling
into the parking lot of the Inn, she experienced a rush
of nervous excitement. Again she glanced at Zebulon.
The emotion was coming from him. Clearly this meeting was of some importance to her client.

Betty Truesdale was sitting behind the tall oak reception desk doing some paperwork when Felicity and
Zebulon entered. "Evening," the middle-aged widow
greeted them with a friendly smile.

Strong waves of curiosity emitted from the proprietress. Felicity blocked them out. For whatever purpose Zebulon had brought her here, she needed to keep
her senses as clear as possible.

"Mr. Carver and his son are waiting for you in the front parlor." Betty indicated the room with a wave of her hand. "You may close the doors if you want privacy."

Felicity returned the woman's smile. "Thank you."

Zebulon merely gave a cursory nod then headed across the hall.

To Felicity's surprise, he paused at the door of the room to wait for her before entering. Then stepping aside, he allowed her to enter ahead of him. A close to overwhelming sense of anticipation greeted her. It wasn't her own.

Her gaze went immediately to the man, with the boy seated on his knee, in the large upholstered chair beside the sofa. They were the same duo she'd seen that afternoon and they were clearly related. Both had the same blond hair and blue eyes. And, although the boy's features were softly defined and the man's more angularly mature, the proportions were the same. In time, both would look even more alike.

The boy, as she had told her grandmother, was cute. The man was handsome. Well, maybe not by everyone's standards, she amended, but certainly by hers, the sight of him igniting an unexpected heat within her. It had been a long time since she'd experienced such an instantly strong attraction. In fact, she'd never experienced anything quite like this before.

As if he felt her eyes on him, he glanced her way and cocked an eyebrow questioningly. She couldn't believe she'd been so obvious about his attractiveness. Stop drooling, she ordered herself. She'd learned her lesson the hard way about men and she had no intention of applying for a refresher course.

Returning to her inspection, she guessed the boy's age at around four and the man to be in his early thirties. The boy looked healthy and well cared for. The man, too, looked exceptionally healthy. A renewed rush of heated excitement raced through her. No! she admonished her traitorous body, ordering herself to ignore this unwanted reaction.

The man stood the boy on the floor and rose. He towered over her five-foot-five frame and she wished she'd taken the time to change into a suit so she could have worn high heels. Her grandfather had taught her that in any confrontation being able to meet a man eye to eye was always an advantage. In this case, even in heels that would have been impossible but at least she would have been a little closer to her goal. Pushing aside her own discomfort, she noted that the anticipation she'd sensed when she entered the room had changed to a guardedness.

Suddenly a strong wave of distrust buffeted her. Instinct guided her gaze to the child. He'd moved slightly, easing himself behind his father. She smiled reassuringly but the distrust remained clearly evident in his eyes.

"I needed someone to drive me here," Zebulon said as he closed the door. His tone suggested that being his chauffeur was the only reason for Felicity's presence.

The man remained standing. "Have you remembered any family history that might help me?" he asked stiffly.

Felicity sensed his irritation at her presence. Hoping to make herself more unobtrusive, she quietly seated herself in a wing chair by the window.

The little boy, she noticed, had turned his full attention to Zebulon but she did not sense the fear most children usually exhibited when encountering the crotchety old man. Instead she read fascination and interest on this child's face.

"Felicity," Zebulon suddenly spoke her name. "This is Lucas Carver and his son, Mark. They claim to be Lanskys." He extracted a photograph yellowed with age. "What do you think?"

So much for trying to be unobtrusive, she mused dryly, accepting the ancient photograph. "Mr. Carver and his son bear a remarkable resemblance to the man in this picture," she said after a moment of scrutiny.

Zebulon returned the photograph to his pocket, then eyed Lucas skeptically. "That picture is of me in my younger days. But by all the records ever kept of our family, I'm the last of the Lanskys."

Lucas's shoulders straightened. "I never said my kin was born on the right side of the blanket."

The excitement Felicity had perceived emitting from Zebulon in the car was once again strong but the old man's demeanor remained stern. "And just whose bed might that blanket have been on?"

The image of a brick wall suddenly flashed in front of Felicity's eyes. She'd sensed people suddenly attempting to shield their secrets but she'd never visualized the actual shield before.

Lucas reached down and in a protective, reassuring gesture, ruffled his son's hair. "My heritage is unimportant. I haven't come here seeking to be declared your kin. I merely want information to help my son."

Felicity sensed a love between the man and boy that held no reservations. It was as strong and pure an emotion as any she'd ever encountered. Momentarily her full attention was fixed on Mark. Whatever was wrong with him, she hoped he could be helped. He suddenly turned to her. The distrust was still in his eyes but there was curiosity as well.

Felicity could see nothing wrong with him. However, the child was obviously in need of some sort of aid. Her instincts assured her that Lucas Carver would never have come to Smytheshire otherwise.

Her gaze shifted to Zebulon. If he had information that could be of use, she didn't understand why he simply didn't give it. But then no one had ever been able to predict Zebulon's behavior much less explain it. Still, she'd never known him to be deliberately cruel.

"There is some knowledge that must be carefully guarded," Zebulon replied. "Until I'm assured of your identity, I cannot help you."

"You will not help me." Lucas corrected him.

Zebulon shrugged. "Cannot...will not. It's all a matter of semantics."

"There are other lives involved."

Felicity felt Lucas's inner struggle almost as if it was her own. The strength of her empathy with this man surprised her.

"You have my word that whatever you tell me will be kept in the strictest confidence," Zebulon assured him.

Lucas turned to Felicity. "What I have to say, I will only say in private."

The "get out of here and close the door after you" was clear in his voice. For the child's sake, Felicity wanted to comply, but Zebulon was her client. She looked to him for her orders.

The old man held up his hand like a traffic cop stopping traffic to let her know he wanted her to stay where she was. "Felicity is my lawyer. Whatever you have to say to me can be said in front of her," he informed Lucas.

Lucas's gaze swung back to Felicity. The thought that she didn't look like a lawyer flashed into her mind. For a moment she was shaken by how clear his impression of her had been, then she frowned at herself. She was overreacting. She'd been thinking that same thought herself. "If you'd like to see a business card..." she offered, reaching for her purse.

Lucas took the card. Felicity Burrow, Attorney at Law, it read, along with an address and phone number. His gaze raked over her. He hadn't needed the card to confirm that she was Zebulon's lawyer. He'd known the old man was telling the truth. Still, the announcement had come as a shock. "Do you prefer to be addressed as Miz, Miss, or is it Missus?" he asked.

Felicity had been scrutinized before, much longer and much more intently, but she'd never felt so completely inspected. "Miss is fine," she replied, her cool mask of authority hiding the disconcerting effect his gaze was having on her. When he turned his attention back to Zebulon, she studied Lucas Carver more closely. There were worry lines in his face and tired ones around his eyes.

"I'm going to sit down," Zebulon announced, lowering himself onto the sofa. "It's been a long day and these old legs are a mite tired."

Lucas eased his son out from behind him and again seated himself in the chair. But as he started to lift the boy onto his lap, Mark gave him a small smile then gently pulled away. To Felicity's surprise, the boy climbed onto the other end of the sofa from where he watched Zebulon with continued interest.

Felicity reckoned there wasn't another child in town who would have been so bold. Zebulon had a natural gruffness about him that did not invite friendly advances. Of course, she observed, the child hadn't sat down right next to the old man. He was keeping a certain amount of distance between them.

"You were going to tell me just how we're related," Zebulon said when the silence that had fallen over the room continued to lengthen.

Felicity noted Lucas's hesitation and sensed renewed inner turmoil, then he said curtly, "My great-grandmother was Linette Molieau."

Zebulon sat bolt upright. "She's still alive?" he asked harshly.

Lucas studied the old man grimly. "No. Lettie passed away a month ago."

Felicity's hands fastened on the arms of her chair as a wrenching wave of grief emitting from Zebulon buffeted her. For the first time, it dawned on her just how attuned she was to the old man. His moods had always been easier for her to read than those of others. Until Lucas Carver had arrived, she amended. She seemed to be unusually attuned to his moods, as well, and she could read his son fairly easily.

His grief hidden, Zebulon met Lucas's gaze levelly. "How did you find out about me?"

"It was a deathbed confession," Lucas said bluntly. "My mother, my maternal grandmother, myself and my son are the only ones who know the truth. Lettie said she was telling us because of concern for my son. I think it was also, at least, partially because she was a decent and honest woman and the secret was tormenting her."

Zebulon scowled. "She had my child and never told me."

"She loved her husband. He wanted a child, and she wanted to give him one. By the time she met you, she was certain that either she was barren or he was sterile.

She had the affair hoping to get pregnant and she did. That was when she sent you away.''

Zebulon's anger flared. ''She used me!''

''Not entirely. She admitted that she had cared for you, even loved you. But she loved her husband as well. For her there was no choice. She was married to Andre Molieau and, in the beginning, her purpose had been to provide him with a child. Her honor insisted that she not veer from her original path. Her suspicion that Andre was incapable of bearing children proved to be true. Your child was the only one she ever conceived.''

Zebulon continued to regard Lucas narrowly. ''You didn't name Andre as among those who know the truth.''

''He died many years ago.''

Zebulon sank back into the sofa. ''Linette Molieau was the only woman I ever loved.'' Suddenly he again sat bolt upright, as a realization struck him. ''Your grandmother is my daughter.''

Lucas nodded.

''What is her name?''

''Camille.''

Zebulon smiled. ''Camille.'' Abruptly the smile was gone. ''How did she take the news of her illegitimacy?''

''She's a strong woman. At first she was shocked. She'd loved her father. He was very good to her. But she also realizes that without you, she would never have come into existence.''

''She would be around seventy-four now,'' Zebulon said, his mind seemingly a million miles away. Then abruptly, his attention snapped back to the present. ''I would like to see her and your mother as well.''

Lucas's jaw firmed. "They knew when I came on this quest that you might feel that way. They are not opposed to meeting with you, but I ask you to be discreet for their sakes."

Zebulon nodded. "I have no desire to interfere with their lives or embarrass them."

Relief showed on Lucas's face. "Lettie said you were a decent man."

Using the arm of the sofa, Zebulon levered himself to his feet. "Come to my place tomorrow morning. We'll talk more then."

Lucas was on his feet, blocking the old man's exit. "Can you help my son?" he demanded.

Felicity was as aware of his parental protectiveness as if it were a physical force.

"Perhaps," Zebulon replied. "Tomorrow. My place."

Lucas glared at the old man. "Why not now?"

Felicity was now sensing Lucas's frustration so strongly, she had to bite her lip to keep from trying to coax Zebulon into complying with his request. Forcefully, she reminded herself that Zebulon was her client and it was his wishes she was there to see were respected.

Zebulon's shoulders squared with resolve. "Tomorrow. My place."

For a moment Lucas looked as if he was going to argue, then obviously realizing it would be futile, he took a step back. "Tomorrow."

Felicity had risen, prepared to intercede if Lucas had not conceded to her client's wishes. A prickling on her neck caused her to glance to the sofa. Mark, too, was now standing but instead of going to his father's side, he was watching her with guarded interest. She gave him an encouraging smile and a wink.

He grinned and winked back. In the next instant, as if worried that he should not have been so friendly, his grin vanished and he hurried to his father.

Zebulon was already in the hall. Felicity started to follow, but paused beside the tall blond man and his son. "I'm sorry Zebulon is being difficult," she said. "But that's his way. People here are used to it. I'm sure that if he can help you, he will."

Lucas looked at her, anger in his eyes. "I will find out what I need to know with his help or without it."

Felicity felt herself being drawn into those blue depths, joining him in his fury. This is his anger, not mine, she reminded herself curtly. And she was not certain if it was even being fairly directed at Zebulon. "I realize you are concerned about your son but I will not allow you to bully my client." Having issued this warning, she strode out of the room.

In the car, driving out of town, Mark's image taunted her. He'd looked perfectly healthy to her but clearly there was something serious enough wrong with him to have caused an old woman to reveal a secret she'd kept for nearly three-quarters of a century and to send Lucas Carver here to Smytheshire. "Would I be overstepping my bounds if I was to ask what is wrong with Mr. Carver's son?"

"He doesn't speak. T'ain't mute. Laughs and cries according to the father. Just won't talk. Doctors can't figure out why."

Felicity glanced at her passenger. "Can you help him?"

"Maybe."

Felicity recalled the brief grin the young boy had cast her way. The memory caused a warm glow within her. "I hope you can," she said.

Zebulon didn't answer. She sensed deep regret and sorrow from him. Her instincts told her he was thinking of the woman he'd known so many years ago. Out of respect, she remained silent for the remainder of the drive.

"What did you think of the lady lawyer?" Lucas asked his son as he tucked Mark into bed.

The boy gave a noncommittal shrug.

Lucas frowned thoughtfully. "I have the strongest feeling I've seen her before."

Pushing off his covers, Mark stood on his bed. Acting as if he were holding something long and about the width of a stick, he began to making digging motions.

Immediately, Lucas recalled where he'd seen Miss Felicity Burrow before. "She's Zebulon's neighbor, the one we saw standing by her porch when we first drove past and later she was hoeing her garden."

Mark grinned triumphantly and nodded vigorously.

Lucas was surprised that he and his son had recognized her from such a brief, distant view. But, hoping not to get lost, he had been very aware of his surroundings as he sought Zebulon's place. Clearly Mark had also been sharply attuned to their search.

"At first glance she looks like the sweet little innocent girl-next-door type," he mused, again tucking his son back into bed. "But that's a deceptive impression." A dry grin tilted one corner of his mouth. "There was a fire in her eyes when she stood up to me. She could be a formidable opponent."

The boy frowned in puzzlement.

"You're right. For me to already think of her as an opponent isn't fair. She did seem to want Zebulon to help us."

His expression solemn, Mark nodded in agreement.

Wandering over to the window, Lucas looked out at the night sky and recalled something else he was certain he'd sensed about Felicity Burrow. She'd been attracted to him.

In his mind's eye he again saw her standing in front of him. He liked her face. She was attractive in a comfortable, wholesome way. Then there was her figure. She definitely had curves in all the right places. He visualized himself combing his fingers into her hair, drawing her toward him and kissing her. The image aroused him. He scowled at himself. He was on an important mission that would not be deterred by a pretty face and a cute figure. Still, as he turned back to the interior of the room, he heard himself saying, "Zebulon does have a good-looking lawyer, don't you think?"

Mark's expression became guarded and again he gave a noncommittal shrug.

Lucas sighed tiredly. "Go to sleep," he said gently. "Tomorrow could be an important day."

A few minutes later, as Lucas climbed into bed, he glanced across the room at his sleeping son. He'd been having one-sided conversations with the boy for so long now they seemed normal. And he'd learned to read his son well. In most instances, he could guess correctly the first time what the boy was thinking. But Mark needed to learn to communicate with others. With a silent prayer that the old man could be of some help, he slept.

Felicity was sitting in one of the rocking chairs on her front porch. The day had seemed endless and she was tired. She'd showered and dressed for bed as soon as she'd arrived home. But she could not get Lucas Carver and his son out of her mind. She'd tossed restlessly in her bed for a while, then come out onto the porch, hoping the soft night would relax her.

She was half-asleep, rocking gently when Lucas Carver's image came suddenly strongly into her mind. He combed his fingers into her hair and kissed her. Her legs felt weak and desire, so strong she could barely breathe, swept through her. Then the image was gone. Shaken, she came fully awake. "Clearly I need a vacation," she muttered. "Or maybe this is nature's way of telling me I should start dating again."

Hurtful memories assailed her. "No," she declared firmly and went inside and to bed.

Chapter Three

"Mutt, go lay down under that tree," Zebulon ordered his dog, using a wave of his arm to indicate the ancient oak standing alone in the clearing in front of his house.

Slowly the dog rose from its stretched-out position beside the old man's rocking chair and lumbered off the porch and into the shade of the tree.

Zebulon's tone and manner softened uncharacteristically as he turned to the blond-haired boy sitting on his father's knee. "Would you keep Mutt company for me while I talk to your dad? He knows you're friends now."

For a moment Mark hesitated, then with an encouraging smile from Lucas, he slipped down and happily hurried to seat himself beside the dog.

"Sometimes children repeat things they hear before they realize it might be best not to tell all they know," Zebulon said by way of explanation.

Lucas had guessed the old man's purpose and nodded. He'd called Zebulon at eight this morning to find out when they could meet. Zebulon had been up and invited him to come whenever he wished. Forty minutes later, Lucas and Mark had been on the old man's doorstep. The past ten minutes, while they'd said their hellos, determined that Lucas didn't want a cup of coffee and gotten the dog and boy out of the way, Lucas's tension had grown. He'd been sensing an uneasiness from the old man and was worried Zebulon might change his mind about revealing whatever it was he knew.

"If you have any information I can give the doctors that might help my son, I'd appreciate you telling me," he coaxed, barely able to hide his impatience.

"I don't know as what I've got to say will be of any use to any doctors," Zebulon replied. "Fact is, it might be best if you keep most of what I'm going to tell you to yourself."

"I give you my word I won't publicly divulge any family secrets that could prove embarrassing to you," Lucas assured him.

Zebulon chuckled. "Oh, there's nothing you could tell people that would embarrass me. But you might cause some others a bit of nervousness."

"I will be discreet." With this second assurance, Lucas noted that Zebulon began to relax, clearly becoming more comfortable with his decision to tell what he knew. In fact, an excitement began to glisten in the old man's eyes. A prickling on the side of Lucas's neck caused him to glance at his son. Mark was watching them expectedly. He gave him a reassuring wink and the boy returned to petting the dog.

"Do you know anything about the Druids?" Zebulon asked.

Surprised by the question, Lucas jerked his attention back to the old man. "My history is a little rusty. I think they were a pre-Christian pagan people, Celtic in origin, killed off centuries ago," he replied, wondering why the old man had asked but deciding he would humor him with an answer.

"The Druids were the members of the priesthood of their society." Zebulon corrected him, then added, "Legend has it that the sorcerer Merlin of the King Arthur tales was of Druid ancestry."

Lucas's patience grew thin. "I don't understand what legends or extinct people have to do with my son."

"The Druids were believed to have powers greater than those of the average man. Some were said to be healers, others were believed to have possessed great mental strengths, strengths that allowed them to move objects with their minds. Some were thought to be able to see into the future. They had the kind of talent people today label as extrasensory powers. And you're right, because of these talents, their conquerors feared them enough to attempt to exterminate them completely. The history books tell us this campaign of extinction succeeded. But you shouldn't always believe everything you read." The excitement in Zebulon's eyes grew more intense. "The Lansky clan can trace its origins back to those ancient Druids."

Lucas began to suspect the old man was a brick short of a full load. "Are you saying that you think the reason my son doesn't talk is because he inherited some magical power?" he demanded, his frustration mingling with anger at this futile waste of time.

Zebulon frowned impatiently. "There's nothing magic about any of the abilities I described. They're merely talents. In their own way, they are no different from those innate talents with which athletes, singers and dancers, for example, are born. They're just different. Instead of inheriting an extraordinary physical skill, our ancestors provided us with the possibility of inheriting an extraordinary mental skill. It's as simple as that."

Lucas's jaw tensed. Coming here had been nothing more than a wild-goose chase. He rose to leave.

Zebulon laid a restraining hand on his arm. "I ain't saying the boy doesn't talk because of some gift he inherited," the old man continued. "Could be, like I said yesterday, he just ain't got nothing to say."

Zebulon's gaze shifted to the boy and the dog. Mark had risen and was starting toward his father, fear and worry written on his face. "Go on back and play with Mutt," Zebulon ordered gently. "Your dad and I aren't finished."

Mark stopped and looked to his father.

"You've come a long way to see me, you might as well hear me out," Zebulon said, giving Lucas's arm a pull to indicate he wanted the man to sit back down.

To Lucas's surprise, his instincts encouraged him to stay. I must be getting really desperate if I have the urge to listen to this old lunatic, he thought, but heard himself saying to Mark, "Go back and sit with Mutt."

"First I'm going to tell you a bit of history that isn't in the books," Zebulon continued as Lucas returned to his chair. "When the conquerors came, the Druids knew they were in danger of extinction. As their strongholds fell, some managed to escape. They fled to other countries, assimilating themselves into those cultures. For safety's sake, most chose not to pass the knowledge of their roots on to their offspring. Instead they allowed their children and their children's children to grow up ignorant of their true heritage."

"But you aren't ignorant of yours?" Lucas was trying to be polite but having a hard time hiding his skepticism.

"No." Zebulon smiled conspiratorially. "I'm not and neither was Angus Smythe, the founder of Smytheshire. The Smythes, unbeknownst to the others, kept track of many of those who fled. Twice in the next centuries, they attempted to gather their Druid brethren together and begin a new community. Each time they failed . . . once because of the suspicions and fears of outsiders and once because of internal strife. Then toward the end of the eighteen hundreds, Angus came to this valley and sought out my grandfather and my father. The Lanskys and the Smythes had kept in contact from one generation to the next and each knew the other knew the secret of their heritage."

Lucas studied Zebulon closely. Clearly the old man believed every word he was saying. He'd obviously been out in these woods by himself too long, Lucas decided.

"The decision to try to bring the community together again was made. Only this time, it was agreed that their Druid heritage would never be mentioned. Angus was a wealthy man. He bought up a huge chunk of land hereabouts and set about building a town. He sought out the people he wanted to settle here. The easiest ones were those who were businessmen working for someone else. He'd say he'd heard they were honest and reliable and he'd explain that he was starting a town he hoped would prosper and offer to loan them the money to set themselves up in business if they'd con-

sider moving to Smytheshire. Then there were those he
invented distant relatives for. He'd contact them and tell
them that they'd inherited land or sometimes even land
and homes here. He was real inventive. I don't think
anyone guessed they'd been singled out special by him.
It was his hope that simply having so many with Druid
genes together in the same locale would cause any ves-
tiges of the power once possessed by our ancestors to
emerge."

Wondering how far the old man went with this fantasy, Lucas became uneasy as he pictured Zebulon in a
hooded long robe chanting over an open fire. "Do you
practice any of the ancient rituals?" he asked bluntly,
intending to leave immediately and advise his mother
and grandmother never to have anything to do with the
old man if the answer was yes.

Zebulon laughed. "No. No. My daddy raised me to
be a God-fearing man. Those old rituals belong to the
days of paganism. In reality they merely served to keep
the Druids' followers in line. You can't get the power
nor, if you have it, can you enhance it by performing a
ritual. Either you're born with it or you're not."

Mentally, Lucas breathed a sigh of relief. At least
Zebulon's fantasies were harmless. "And were you born
with one of these talents?"

Zebulon shook his head. "No, not me. At least, not
as I've noticed." The old man's eyes again glistened and
he lowered his voice conspiratorially. "But there are
some here who have exhibited a touch of talent. Nothing spectacular, mind you." He paused for a moment
and frowned thoughtfully. "Although there was one
incident a long time ago. Zachariah Gerard—"
Abruptly he stopped and shook his head as if worried

this could be a faulty account. "Nope. Can't say as I've ever actually seen anything really astonishing."

Lucas frowned at himself. He couldn't believe he was listening to this insanity. When he'd arrived in Smythe-shire, he'd sensed a comfortableness about the town. The place had the feel of old-fashioned Americana where neighbor helped neighbor. It was the kind of town he'd always thought he would enjoy living in. He had, in fact, experienced a curious sensation very akin to that of arriving home after a long journey. And his first encounters with Zebulon had left him with the impression that the man was cautious and distrusting of strangers but certainly sane. How he could have been so wrong on both counts surprised him. His first reaction to people and places was usually more reliable. "Do you have psychic gatherings on the courthouse lawn?" he asked wryly, his tone mocking both the old man's tale and himself for listening to it.

Zebulon scowled. "The people in this town ain't sideshow freaks. Like I said, as far as I know, most don't even know about their ancestry. Them that do ain't claiming it. They go about their lives just like nor-mal, everyday people. Those with a talent don't even realize they have it and, if they do, they sure don't flaunt it. You tell anyone in town what I just told you and they'll most likely think you belong in a loony bin."

Zebulon's scowl deepened. "Take Wanda Elberly, for instance, and those crystals of hers. The first ones were given to her by her great-grandmother because she told the old lady she heard them singing. But no one else has ever claimed to hear them singing and her insistence that they did embarrassed her family mightily. Her mother explained it away by saying the child had a strong imagination and was always humming a tune to herself. Now everyone blames Wanda's hearing aids for being faulty. I figure her great-grandmother used to hear them but was smart enough to keep her mouth shut. And Wanda did stop talking about them when she reached her teens and never mentioned the singing again until she was in her fifties. T'ain't fun to be the brunt of jokes and having people look at you as if your head wasn't on quite straight.''

This conversation was going nowhere that made any sense, Lucas groaned mentally. It was time to go. "I appreciate what you've told me," he said, keeping his tone polite. Zebulon was old, and there was no use upsetting the old man because of a few harmless fantasies he'd built up through the years.

As Lucas rose, Zebulon rose also. "I can tell you think my head might not be on any straighter than Wanda's," the old man said. "But if you're really looking for answers, there is one person you should see before you leave town."

"I really don't think anyone here can help my son," Lucas replied, thinking that every family has its eccentrics and he'd definitely found the one in his.

"Celina Prescott can't cure the boy but she can tell if those fancy doctors of yours have missed anything," Zebulon persisted.

I draw the line at taking my son to a fortune teller, Lucas declared mentally. Aloud, he merely said politely, "Unless she's a doctor, I don't think she can help."

Zebulon remained persistent. "She's married to a doctor, a good one, at that. Took over as the town doctor when Doc James retired. But that's neither here nor there. It's my guess her ancestors were healers."

"I really have to be going." Lucas started to step off the porch.

"If you're as concerned as you say about the boy, you'd be smart to hear me out," Zebulon warned.

Lucas turned back to face him. "I'm not so desperate I'd place my son in the hands of a quack."

"Celina is not a quack." Zebulon caught Lucas by the arm and locked his gaze on the younger man's as if trying to will him to believe him. "When she was young, she and her parents were in a plane crash. She was the only survivor, but the injuries she suffered left her deaf. Since then, she's been able to tell if there was something wrong inside a person's body by touching them. Doc James told me she says she feels a heat over the spot where there's something amiss. She don't know what the problem is but she can tell a doctor where to look." Again a twinkle showed in his eyes. "Sounds a bit like some of that newfangled technology I've been reading about, only in this case you've got human sensitivities giving it a bit of fine-tuning."

Lucas forced himself to keep his voice polite. "I think I'll stick to more conventional diagnostic techniques."

Mark had joined his father and was looking from one man to the other with a worried expression.

"Seems to me those conventional methods haven't been too successful," Zebulon observed. Releasing his hold on Lucas, he ruffled Mark's hair and his gaze softened. "This here is my great-great-grandson. I wouldn't suggest anything I thought would harm him."

Lucas did not doubt that the old man truly cared for the boy. But that didn't mean Zebulon had a firm grasp on reality. "I'll think about it," he said, wanting merely to get away from there without upsetting Zebulon further.

As Lucas took Mark by the hand and started to head to their rental car, Zebulon again laid a restraining hand on Lucas's arm. "I'd still like to see my daughter and granddaughter. But I'll leave that up to them. If they're willing to meet with me, have them write or call and name a time and place. You have my address and my phone number. Even if they'd rather I didn't show my face in their lives, I'd like to hear from you again. Just a note once in a while to let me know how you're doing."

Releasing Lucas, he again ruffled Mark's hair. "My great-great-grandson," he murmured. Then his gaze again turned to Lucas. "Take care of yourself and your boy. I know what I've told you seems a might farfetched but there are many strange things in this world. You should keep an open mind."

Again, Lucas could not deny the honesty in the old man's expressed concern for himself and his son. His instincts also assured him that Zebulon would keep his word and not contact either Lucas's mother or grandmother without their consent. "I'll keep in touch," he promised. He wasn't sure why he'd made that pledge. Zebulon's ladder was obviously missing a rung or two and he wasn't so sure the old man would be a good influence on his son. The last thing he wanted was for Mark's mind to be filled with fanciful legends. But Zebulon Lansky was family, Lucas reminded himself, and he'd always felt strongly about family ties.

Zebulon nodded in gratitude.

Lucas took out his wallet and extracted a business card. On the back he wrote his home phone number. "Contact me if you ever need me."

Reading the front of the card, Zebulon grinned. "Vice president of a bank," he said with approval.

Mark touched the old man's hand.

"It's his way of saying goodbye," Lucas explained when Zebulon looked down questioningly at the boy.

Zebulon winked at the child. "You come back."

Mark nodded.

His son truly liked the old man, Lucas realized and was forced to admit that he did, too. When a person nears a hundred years of age, they're entitled to be a little eccentric, he reasoned.

"If you should decide to contact Celina you'd be wise to do it through Felicity. Celina's real good at reading lips but just to be on the safe side, you should have someone along who knows how to sign. Besides, I don't know how Celina would take to a stranger asking her to use her talent, and I ain't too good about dealing with the townsfolk, especially the women." Zebulon's gaze suddenly became misty. "Your great-grandmother was one of the few women I ever felt comfortable with."

"I'll keep that in mind," Lucas replied, thinking it would be a cold day in hell before he sought out this Celina person's help.

Pulling out onto the main road a few minutes later, he glanced toward his son apologetically. "I'm afraid this was a wild-goose chase."

Mark gave no indication he'd even heard. Instead he continued to gaze expectantly out the windshield. Lucas was wondering what the boy had on his mind when he saw Mark sit up straighter for a better view. They rounded a bend and the Burrow's house came into view.

The old woman who had been sitting on the porch the afternoon before was in her rocking chair. She waved as they passed and Mark waved back, but Lucas saw the

disappointment on his son's face as the boy sank back
into his seat. "The lady lawyer was sort of interesting," he said, continuing to study Mark out of the corner of his eye.

The boy nodded, then frowned as if angry with himself for having been looking for her.

"I suppose we should stop by and see her. I'd like for
her to have our phone number and address just in case
Zebulon should need help of any kind. And, I'd like to
make sure there is someone here in town who keeps an
eye on the old man. After all, he is family."

Mark nodded his agreement. It was definitely a cautious nod, Lucas noted. Still, it was a nod. He frowned
thoughtfully. Mark was generally withdrawn around
women near his mother's age. In fact, Felicity Burrow
was the very first in this category he'd ever appeared to
want to seek out.

Chapter Four

Felicity rose and rounded her desk as Lucas Carver and his son entered her office. She'd been surprised when Peggy Cassidy, her secretary, had buzzed her and announced their arrival.

"I hope we're not interrupting anything important," Lucas apologized, extending his hand.

"No, not at all." Accepting the handshake, Felicity was, as she had been last night, acutely aware of the man's inspection. Today, however, she knew she looked like a lawyer. Her hair was brushed into a stylish sweep away from her face. A light coating of makeup gave her a more mature air. Finally she was clothed in a gray suit worn with a pale pink silk blouse and matching gray heeled shoes. Taken all together, she looked efficient and businesslike.

Inside was a different matter. She'd woken with the same restlessness she'd experienced yesterday. And as Lucas's gaze traveled over her, it felt very close to a physical touch. He didn't leer. His expression was, in fact, coolly polite. Yet she was certain he liked what he saw and that simple knowledge caused a stirring of arousal. I definitely need a vacation, she told herself. Aloud, she said, "How can I help you?"

The curve of her hips were causing lecherous thoughts to play through Lucas's mind. You're thinking like a teenager in heat, he chided himself and jerked his attention back to his reason for being there. "I wanted to leave my address with you. I'd appreciate it if you'd contact me if Zebulon should ever need any help."

As he took out a business card, he glanced down at his son to see Mark studying the female lawyer.

Felicity's gaze, too, turned to the young boy. He obviously found her interesting and this, she sensed, seemed to surprise the father. While Lucas jotted down his home address and phone number on the back of his business card, she squatted in front of Mark to bring herself to his eye level. "I see you met Mutt," she said, brushing a few dog hairs from his shirt.

He flinched back as if she'd struck him.

"Sorry," she apologized quickly. Obviously she'd stepped over a line she was not supposed to cross.

He grimaced self-consciously, then stepped forward and touched her face. It was like a caress and she knew he was apologizing to her. Then he stepped back until he was half-hidden behind his father's leg.

Felicity suddenly found herself forgetting the boy as her gaze traveled along the sturdy column of Lucas Carver's jeans encased leg to his flat abdomen. Sensual thoughts swirled in her head. Quickly she straightened to her full height, her expression one of cool command belying the fire that threatened to ignite within her.

Felicity's sudden apology to Mark had caused Lucas to glance down at the woman to make certain there was not a problem. His view had given him a hint of cleavage and he'd found himself wondering how her breasts would feel cupped in his hands. Get your mind back to business, he ordered himself as she straightened. Extending the business card toward her, he said, "I know Zebulon is a little loony but he is family."

Felicity frowned. "Zebulon Lansky might be a bit cantankerous and standoffish, but he's one of the sanest men I know."

Obviously she hadn't been treated to Zebulon's version of the Lansky family history nor the founding of Smytheshire, Lucas mused. Deciding that keeping that information to himself would be wise, he still felt the need to challenge her trust in Zebulon. "He suggested I take my son to see some woman by the name of Celina Prescott."

Felicity continued to frown as she looked down at the boy who had come out from behind his father's leg and was now studying her again. "Zebulon told me about the basis of your concern for your son. I suppose you've had tests run?"

"Every one in the book," Lucas replied, placing a protective hand on Mark's shoulder.

Felicity's gaze shifted to the father. "Celina can't cure him," she said bluntly. "But there have been times when she's found something the doctors have missed." She grimaced self-consciously. "Well, not exactly 'found,' either. She can only tell the doctors where to take a closer look."

Was this whole town as dotty as his great-grandfather? Lucas wondered. "You honestly believe she's some sort of psychic diagnostician?"

Felicity scowled at his ridiculing tone. "I'm not saying she is, and she's never claimed to be perfect. She always insists people go see a doctor."

"I suppose that bodes well for her husband then," he returned cynically. "I understand he's the doctor in town."

"From what I've heard, Reid Prescott was as skeptical as you when he first met her." Felicity read the look in Lucas's eyes easily. He was thinking that maybe she was as daft as he thought Zebulon was. Her shoulders stiffened. "No one's claiming she can work miracles." Her manner became cool with dismissal. "I'm sure Zebulon was simply trying to be helpful. Good day." Turning away, she rounded her desk.

"Good day," he replied to her back.

She seated herself in time to see the door closing behind them. Still holding the business card in her hands, she frowned at the front of it. Mr. Lucas Carver was vice president of a bank in Seattle, Washington. A good occupation for a close-minded man with no imagination, she thought dryly, rising to file the card in Zebulon's folder.

As Lucas stepped off the porch of the small, well-kept, single-story, white-shingled building in which Burrow and Burrow, Attorneys-at-Law, was housed, he noticed his son glancing back. There was an unhappy expression on the boy's face.

"Maybe I was a little judgmental," he admitted. "I know some very sane people who read their horoscopes every day. And there are some very prominent people who consult psychics on a regular basis." And I am getting pretty desperate, he added to himself. Very desperate, he amended. "I suppose it couldn't hurt to have this Celina person take a look at you."

The boy glanced up at him dubiously.

"That'd give us a chance to apologize to Miss Burrow and maybe get back on her good side," Lucas coaxed. To himself, he admitted a surprise that this mattered so much to him.

Mark looked over his shoulder at the door through which they had just exited. For a moment he hesitated, then he smiled tentatively and nodded his agreement.

Going back inside, Lucas smiled at the pleasant looking, middle-aged woman seated behind the desk in the reception area. "I was wondering if we could have a few minutes more of Miss Burrow's time."

As Peggy Cassidy punched the intercom button on her phone and announced their return, Lucas wondered if he was about to be thrown out. Behind her cool facade, Miss Felicity Burrow had been angry...very angry. That he knew without a doubt.

"You may go in," Peggy said.

Lucas sensed that she was curious but it was a deeply buried curiosity, one that was clearly kept under tight control. An excellent secretary for a lawyer, he judged. Aloud, he said, "Thank you," and guided his son back into Felicity's inner sanctum.

This time she did not rise but remained seated behind her desk. "What else can I do for you?" she asked frostily.

"I'll admit that, maybe, I was a bit too skeptical," he said.

His sincerity surprised Felicity. "I can't blame you," she conceded. "Celina's knack does seem farfetched. If I wasn't aware of a couple of incidents where she was actually able to help people, I'd be skeptical myself."

Lucas relaxed. He wasn't sure if this was because she was no longer angry with him or because she was levelheaded, after all, and did not think of this Celina's abilities as a normal, everyday occurrence. Both, he decided. "I am becoming somewhat desperate," he confessed gruffly.

Felicity sensed his embarrassment. She also felt a sharp jolt of apprehension. Her gaze turned to Mark. That last sensation had come from him.

"I've been rethinking my position and have decided that it couldn't do any harm to have Mrs. Prescott take a look at Mark," Lucas continued.

Felicity's attention jerked back to the man. This was a surprise.

"Zebulon suggested that I ask you to accompany me. He explained that Mrs. Prescott is deaf and that she would be cautious of a stranger asking her to use her unique ability. I'll pay you for your time." Even as he completed his request, Lucas felt foolish about having made it. He didn't really believe this Prescott woman could help him. Still, he was unable to stop himself from pursuing this. *I am really grabbing at straws now,* he chided himself.

The jolt of apprehension Felicity had experienced before became a steady flow. She turned to the boy. "There is nothing to fear," she assured him.

Mark visibly relaxed.

That the woman's reassurance had eased his son's mind, startled Lucas. Normally the boy would have turned to him for a second opinion. "Then you will take us to see her?"

"Yes, of course. And at no charge." Felicity wondered why she'd detected a jolt of surprise. Feeling nearly overpowered by the strength of the various emotions stirring in the air, she glanced at her watch, using the diversion to clear her mind. "It's almost noon. We can probably catch her on her lunch break."

As the three left the building, Felicity asked, "Do you want to drive or shall I?"

"You might as well. You know your way around here better than I do," he replied.

"Celina often surprises strangers," Felicity said, pulling onto the street. "She can read lips very well, and because she lost her hearing after she'd learn to speak, she also speaks clearly."

Lucas merely nodded. Sensing that he was not in the mood for conversation, Felicity fell silent. A few minutes later, when she guided her car into the parking lot of the Smytheshire library, he looked at her and raised an eyebrow questioningly.

"Celina is our head librarian," she explained.

Lucas had promised himself that if they parked in front of a house with talismans dangling from the trees or porch roof, he was going to very quickly change his mind about subjecting his son to the scrutiny of Celina Prescott. He still was not completely comfortable about his decision but at least he felt safer. They were in a public place and the woman had to be educated to hold the position she held.

Felicity was again aware of a range of turbulent emotions. Mildly disconcerted by the unusually strong vibes she was receiving from her two companions, she led the way inside.

"Afternoon," Brenda Norwood greeted the trio as they entered. Her gaze immediately focused on Lucas. A quick appraisal brought a glitter of feminine appreciation to her eyes. "I don't believe I've ever seen you in town before."

Felicity felt a small nudge of impatience toward the twenty-four-year-old assistant librarian.

"We're just here on a visit," Lucas replied with a friendly smile. "Felicity is being kind enough to show us around."

Brenda grinned at both Lucas and Felicity. "Lucky her."

"I thought I would introduce him to Celina," Felicity said, having to fight to keep a sharpness out of her voice. She told herself that if the woman wanted to flirt outrageously with a total stranger that was her right. Besides, in fairness, she had to admit that Brenda wasn't really being outrageous. She was merely showing a healthy interest. And I'm overreacting, she added.

"Celina's in her office having lunch with Kenneth," Brenda informed them. Her attention turned to Mark and she gave him a bright smile as well. "We have a terrific nursery room with books for kids your age."

Mark moved into a protected position behind his father as if afraid the librarian would snatch him up and take him to the room she'd just mentioned.

"We'll keep him with us," Lucas said.

"Yes, of course." Brenda continued to smile to let him know she wasn't offended. "I can see he's a little shy. Maybe you'll bring him again, and he'll want to take a look at the books."

Lucas smiled back. "Yes, maybe next time."

Brenda was nearly glowing with pleasure, Felicity observed. Again she experienced a wave of impatience. "We'd better be going," she coaxed, already heading toward the back of the library.

As they passed a windowed door with Storybook Room painted on it in multicolored letters, Lucas glanced inside. It looked like a comfortable nursery.

There were a couple of cribs along one wall. On the other side of the room was a child-size table and chairs and bookshelves full of large picture books. There were even a few toys scattered around. An elderly woman sitting in a chair near the window was reading to several children around Lucas's age. One was on her lap, and the others were gathered in a semicircle around her.

"The Storybook Room was put in after Celina gave birth to Kenneth. She wanted to continue to work but she also wanted her child nearby. It's proved to be a very good way of introducing young children to books," Felicity said, noticing the direction of his attention.

Lucas nodded his approval.

Next came a closed door with Librarian painted on it. Felicity pressed a button. "This causes a light to blink off and on inside," she explained.

The door opened and Lucas found himself looking at a pleasant-faced, pregnant, auburn-haired woman with brown eyes and a polite smile, which warmed considerably when she saw Felicity. "How nice to see you." Opening the door fully, she motioned for them to enter.

Seated at a table on the far side of the room, was a child Lucas judged to be a year or so younger than his own son.

"Kenneth and I have just finished lunch," Celina said. She squatted to put herself on eye level with Mark. "There is some lemonade left. Would you like a glass?"

Mark shook his head and again sought refuge behind his father.

Felicity tapped Celina on the shoulder to get her attention. "Actually Mark is the reason we are here," she said, using sign language as well as verbal speech to be certain the librarian understood completely.

Kenneth had wiggled down from his chair and approached Mark. "Hi," he said. "Me Kenneth," he added pointing to himself.

Mark grinned back shyly.

"Me Kenneth," Kenneth repeated, again pointing to himself. Then he pointed at Mark. "Who you?"

Lucas hesitated, knowing his son wouldn't respond and yet hoping he would. When Mark merely regarded the younger child with quiet interest, Lucas said, "His name is Mark." Then turning to face Celina, he explained stiffly, "My son doesn't speak. I've had every test in the book run on him. Zebulon suggested you might be able to tell me if the doctors have missed something."

Celina straightened. "Zebulon Lansky told you to come see me?" she asked, clearly surprised.

"He's a relative of Zebulon's." Felicity spoke up, again signing.

Celina turned her full attention to Felicity. "Did I understand correctly, the boy doesn't speak?"

Felicity nodded and formed the sign for yes.

Celina turned back to Lucas. "I give no guarantees I can be of any help."

He nodded his understanding.

Moving Kenneth just a little and taking his place so she could get a full view of Mark, she again lowered herself to his eye level. "I need to touch you," she said gently.

"My mom," Kenneth said with pride pointing to her and edging closer to her.

Mark looked as if he was going to rebel.

Lucas started to coax his son to cooperate but it was Felicity who spoke up. "It's all right," she said encouragingly. She squatted beside Celina hoping to ease his nervousness. The realization of how much she liked this child shook her. She barely knew him. Still, with every fiber of her being, she hoped Celina could be of some help.

"You're among friends," Lucas told his son.

The boy looked at Felicity. She smiled and a crooked grin started to lift one corner of his mouth.

"Celina is my friend. She wants to help," Felicity coaxed.

For a moment more he continued to hang back, then with a resigned expression, he stepped forward.

"You've got your father's hair and eyes," Celina noted as she gently ran her hands over his head and face then down his neck and over the rest of him. Finishing, she grinned at him. "That wasn't so terrible was it?"

He shrugged and stepped back.

"He feels perfectly healthy to me," Celina said as she straightened.

Felicity gave Mark a wink and was rewarded with another crooked grin. Then she, too, straightened. "Nothing?" she asked, signing the word for emphasis.

Celina shook her head. "Nothing." Her gaze swung back to Lucas. "I have never claimed to be infallible. I hope you will keep seeking an answer."

"I will," Lucas assured her. He thought he'd feel like a fool for having come here but he didn't. Celina Prescott was a nice woman, obviously a motherly one who truly meant well.

"I'm sorry," Felicity said as they left the library a few minutes later.

Lucas shrugged. "I didn't really expect anything. Coming here was merely an act of desperation."

Mark pulled on his hand and pointed to his stomach.

Lucas nodded. "Lunch. Right." The thought of parting company with Felicity caused an unexpectedly strong surge of regret. "Miss Burrow, would you do us the honor of joining us? I feel I owe you something for your time."

Felicity was tempted more than she wanted to admit. The thought of calling Peggy and having her reschedule her next appointment played through her mind. She shoved it out. She wouldn't treat a client like that. Besides, she was attracted to Lucas Carver. She couldn't deny that. No use looking for trouble, she warned herself. As far as she knew, he was a married man and even if he wasn't, she'd sworn off men. Glancing at her watch, she said with apology, "I can't. I have a one o'clock appointment. I'll just have time to get us back to the office and eat my bag lunch."

In spite of the aura of apology around her, Lucas sensed an underlying fear. What, he wondered, had made the lady lawyer so uneasy about a simple luncheon invitation?

A touch on her hand caused Felicity to glance down to see Mark looking at her. There was a plea in his eyes that touched her heart. But she knew trouble when she saw it and Lucas Carver was trouble with a capital *T*. "I'm really sorry, but I can't join you," she said.

Lucas noted that this time there was nothing but pure regret behind her words. A few minutes later, as she parked beside their car, bid them goodbye and went into her office, he found himself unable to pull his gaze away from her until she had closed the door between them. She is an appealing woman, he thought to himself. But maybe her desire to keep a distance between them was good. He would like to find a woman to share his life with, however, he was looking for someone who would

consider her home her career and would be a full-time
mother to his son.

Felicity drew a shaky breath as she entered her office. Glancing in the hall mirror and seeing the flush on
her cheeks, she was grateful Peggy was still on her lunch
break. She'd been aware of Lucas Carver's gaze following her. But the sensation it created was one she'd
never before experienced. It had the effect of an arousing caress. Keeping a distance between herself and that
man had been a wise choice.

But maybe not a fair one, her conscience argued as
she watched from her window while he buckled his son
into their rented car. Last night when she'd told her
grandmother about the boy's condition, she'd learned
that she had not spoken until she was nearly three.

"That's why you had that bit of speech therapy.
When you finally did start talking you began with sen-
tences and ran all your words together so nobody could
tell what you were saying," her grandmother had rem-
inisced.

Maybe her grandmother could offer some sugges-
tions to aid Mark. As Lucas rounded the car, she could
see the small, cute face looking her way. In the next instant, her legs were carrying her out of her office and
out the front door.

She waved Lucas to a stop before he could start the
engine. Don't think about him, she ordered herself
when he stepped out of the car and her blood began to
flow faster. She focused her thoughts on the boy. Coming to a halt a couple of feet from Lucas, she said levelly, "I was wondering if you and Mark would like to
join my grandmother and me for dinner tonight."

Lucas could tell that she was not enthusiastic about
issuing this invitation and he wondered why she had.

But the reason didn't seem to really matter. Neither did the fact that he'd planned on leaving town today. He wanted to see her again. "What time?"

"Six," she replied, then quickly turned and went back inside.

Mark was smiling when his father climbed back into the car.

"So you wanted to see her again, too," Lucas observed.

Mark nodded.

A little later as they sat eating lunch, a thought that had been nagging at the back of Lucas's mind forced itself to the forefront. Maybe he was not being entirely fair to Zebulon. He'd always assumed that his ability to read other peoples emotions was because he'd trained himself to be attuned to the tiny nuances, the body language, that subtly exposed underlying feelings. Now he wondered if maybe this ability was an inborn talent. After all, he'd had it for as long as he could remember.

Abruptly he gave his shoulders a shake. He was not going to be drawn into the old man's fantasy. Tersely he told himself that he was merely more observant of others than most people.

Chapter Five

Felicity came out onto the porch to greet Mark and Lucas as they parked in front of her home. "I hope you're hungry. Grams loves to cook and when I told her I'd invited company, she spent the day in the kitchen."

"Smells delicious," Lucas said, getting a whiff of the aromas floating out of the house. But it wasn't her grandmother's cooking that was arousing his hunger. Instead it was Felicity's lips that were on his mind. Would they taste as sweet as they looked? he wondered.

Unexpectedly picturing herself in Lucas's arms, Felicity forced her attention away from him and to his son. "I hope you like chicken and dumplings and cherry pie. If not, Grams fried a few pieces of chicken and made a chocolate cake as well. Unless you and your dad eat ravenously, I'm going to be having leftovers for the next month."

"Now, don't you fret about leftovers. I can always take a few to Zebulon." Thelma's voice sounded from behind Felicity.

Definitely an old-fashioned grandmother, Lucas judged, his gaze traveling over the short, slightly plump gray-haired woman in the comfortable cotton dress protected by a full apron. Her cheeks were flushed from the heat of her kitchen and her smile was warm and friendly. "I'm Lucas Carver and this is my son, Mark." He extended a hand.

"Thelma Burrow," she replied, accepting the handshake.

Her grip was firm. He liked that. "We appreciate the invitation, Mrs. Burrow."

"Call me Thelma. I'm real glad you could come. I'll admit, I've been sort of curious. Felicity was vague about your relationship to Zebulon, but he walked over this afternoon and told me the whole story." Her smile warmed even more. "But don't you fret, I ain't a gossip. Nobody'll hear anything from me. Guess I'm about the only person hereabouts Zebulon does talk to 'cause he knows I wouldn't go telling anyone." She laughed lightly. "That comes from living in a family of lawyers."

Lucas liked Thelma Burrow. There was no pretense about her.

"Welcome, Mark." Thelma Burrow turned her attention to the boy, extending her hand toward him as she had his father.

Felicity noticed that Mark stepped forward without hesitation. Well, her grandmother had always had a way with children, she recalled.

As Mark accepted the handshake, Thelma said, "Why don't you come inside and help me finish putting dinner together? Felicity and your dad can sit out here and enjoy the evening.''

To Felicity's surprise Mark readily nodded in agreement. She was tempted to insist on helping also. She didn't want to be left alone with Lucas. The sensuous thoughts that kept popping into her head when she was around him were disconcerting. However, she also wanted her grandmother to have some time alone with the boy. Forcing a smile, she watched them go inside.

Again Lucas was aware of her hesitation to be in his company. ''You don't have to be afraid of being alone with me,'' he assured her. ''I don't bite. At least, not viciously.'' Immediately he found himself thinking about nibbling on her earlobe. She might not be the wife he'd envisioned, but Felicity Burrow, he had to admit, was having an unusually strong lusty effect on him.

The thought of him nipping her earlobe played through Felicity's mind causing a rush of heat. Turning to him, she started to deny that he bothered her in any way but the lie seemed too big. Instead she merely shrugged. Then seating herself on the porch swing, she indicated with a small wave of her hand that he was welcome to seat himself in the rocking chair.

For a long moment, Lucas continued to study her. She hadn't denied his accusation. Again, he told himself it would probably be wise to keep a distance between them, but a part of him, something deep inside, refused. It insisted on finding out why she was so uncomfortable in his presence. However, the stern set of her jaw coupled with her reticence suggested it would be prudent to try a little small talk first. ''Beautiful country around here,'' he said, accepting the unspoken invitation.

"Yes, it is." Felicity had been looking toward the road, trying to ignore him. But as he stretched his long legs out in front of him, she caught a glimpse of them out of the corner of her eye. A chill of excitement swept through her and his presence filled her mind. Get a grip! she ordered herself.

Experiencing another flash of lustiness, Lucas glanced toward her. The urge to join her on that swing was close to overwhelming.

Determinedly, Felicity turned her thoughts to Mark. "Grams has always had a knack with children but considering Mark's shyness, I expected him to be a little more standoffish, at least at first."

Another woman's face filled Lucas's mind. A coldness descended over him. "Your grandmother has a comforting manner." He focused on a spot in the distance. "Besides, it's only women around your age...his mother's age...that he's overly cautious about allowing himself to like too swiftly."

Felicity's full attention was on him now. This was the first time he'd mentioned Mark's mother and she had the distinct impression that he disliked that subject. The boy's mother was not her concern, she told herself. Still her curiosity was piqued. "She did not make the trip with you." It was a statement, neither questioning nor laced with any emotion. She'd learned this trick a long time ago. It allowed the responder to tell her as little or as much as he wished without being placed in the position of having to be evasive.

"No, she didn't."

Felicity frowned. She'd given him the option of maintaining his privacy but she'd hoped he'd provide more information. His private life is not my concern, she admonished herself again. Still her curiosity remained. She assured herself she only wanted to know more because of Mark. Maybe the boy's relationship with his mother would help explain his reticence. "I suppose it was wise to keep your first meeting with Zebulon limited to just you and your son."

Lucas didn't like talking about Phyllis, but he found himself disliking keeping secrets from Felicity Burrow even more. That he had this need to be totally open with her shocked him. He was normally more cautious about revealing the less savory portions of his private life until he knew someone a whole lot better.

Felicity sensed a struggle within him, then it was over. Continuing to stare at a point in the distance, he said, "Mark's mother is not a part of our lives. Phyllis is an investment counselor. We had a long-term affair. Her career was the most important thing in her life. She wanted a man she could feel safe with but not committed to. I found her attractive and enjoyable company. The arrangement worked well for both of us. There were no jealous rages."

"Sounds like a practical relationship," Felicity noted, thinking she wouldn't mind that kind of arrangement with him herself. Quickly she shoved the thought from her mind. She knew herself well enough to know that she could never be intimate with a man without an emotional attachment and a romantic emotional attachment was the last thing she wanted.

Lucas frowned. "It was. But accidents happen. Phyllis got pregnant. She had the decency to tell me. Then she said she was going to have an abortion. She said she didn't want to be a mother, she knew she would be lousy at it. I couldn't disagree with her. Her only real love was for money...not the actual physical sub-

stance but the power and excitement she got from ma-
nipulating it.''

Felicity glanced toward the house where Mark was
inside with her grandmother. "But she changed her
mind.''

"Not exactly.'' The frown on Lucas's face deepened.
"I told myself that abortion was the practical solution,
still I wanted the child. I've never wanted anything so
strongly in my life. We cut a deal. We married, she had
the baby, then we divorced. She got a hundred thousand dollars and signed a paper giving me sole custody
of our child. Even before the birth, she'd lined up a job
with a firm in New York. She couldn't wait to put as
much distance between herself and Mark as possible.
We didn't make a good married couple. We were civil
but on a daily basis quickly bored of each other's company.''

His gaze shifted to Felicity. "I love my son. My
mother, my father, and my grandmother dote on him.
My great-grandmother, Lettie, adored him. Even Phyllis's parents are fond of him. They live in Florida but
make an effort to see him at least once a year and always remember him on the holidays and his birthday.
I've tried to convince myself that with all the love Mark
has bestowed on him, his mother's attitude is unimportant. But I can't help wondering if, while he was in the
womb, he sensed she didn't want him and that's why he
doesn't speak. He's always been standoffish around
women her age as if he expects to be rejected by them.''

"It's my guess he's not talking because he doesn't
have to.''

Felicity had become so absorbed in Lucas's concern
for his son, she was startled by the sound of her grandmother's voice.

"I thought you two might like some lemonade while you wait," Thelma said, through the screen door. Before Lucas or Felicity could rise to help, she'd pushed the door open with her elbow and stepped out onto the porch. After handing them each a glass, she gave her full attention to Lucas. "I only caught the last of what you were saying. But in just the short time I've been with your son, I've noticed he's developed a very efficient system of hand signals. And, if I ignore them, he lets out an uncomfortable squeal and does the signal again."

Lucas nodded. "My mother and grandmother have mentioned the same thing. But when we tried to force him to speak to get what he wanted, he would simply decide that whatever it was, was not worth the price or he would attempt to get it himself."

Thelma nodded her understanding. "Felicity didn't speak until she was nearly three."

Lucas's gaze swung to Felicity. So she had exhibited behavior similar to his son's. That could explain the affinity Mark felt toward the lady lawyer. "What made you start?" he demanded gruffly.

"She was always partial to my blueberry cobbler." Thelma spoke up before Felicity had a chance to answer. "One afternoon, her cousin Simon was here. That boy was a human garage disposal. He ate his piece of cobbler then reached for hers. 'Mine,' she said as clearly and distinctly as if she'd been talking for ages. Simon froze in shock. Everyone else sat numb for a moment then Felicity's father applauded and the others followed his example. 'Well, it's about time,' he said."

Felicity flushed with embarrassment. "I guess I realized it was time to stand up for myself."

Grams grinned. "Once that first word was spoken, we couldn't shut her up. She ran her words together so that a single sentence came out as a single word. It was as if she had a lot to say and wanted it to come out all at once. It was quite a jumble for a while but at least she was talking." Her expression became serious. "Maybe Mark simply hasn't found anything he can't live without yet."

"You don't happen to have any blueberry cobbler around, do you?" Lucas asked hopefully.

"I've got something better. I made my prizewinning chocolate cake," she replied with a smile, then went back inside.

As the door closed and they were once again alone on the porch, Lucas turned to Felicity. "Do you think Zebulon remembered about you not speaking and that was why he had you come with him last night, then sent me to you this morning?"

Felicity shrugged. "I don't know. I've learned through the years never to try to second-guess him. But I find it hard to believe that, even if he was aware of my not talking right off, he'd remember something so inconsequential. My own family never mentioned it. In fact, I didn't know until Grams told me last night. I thought I'd had a perfectly normal childhood."

Lucas frowned thoughtfully. "I have a feeling Zebulon keeps a closer eye on the people in this town than anyone realizes."

Felicity looked at him questioningly.

Zebulon's warning to be cautious about telling others his version of the founding of Smytheshire played through Lucas's mind. It wasn't that he'd decided to believe the old man, he assured himself. Still, he chose to keep the confidence. No sense in saying something that would convince Miss Felicity Burrow that he was as loony as he'd suggested Zebulon was. "I guess it's a good thing he's not a gossip," he added flippantly, his tone suggesting his speculation about Zebulon was unimportant.

"I guess so," Felicity replied noncommittally. She had the strongest feeling there was something Lucas wasn't saying. But then she'd learned from experience that no one ever said everything that was on their mind.

"Can I assume it was learning about your own reticence that prompted you to invite Mark and me to dinner tonight?" Lucas turned the conversation back to the reason he'd come to Smytheshire in the first place.

"I was hoping my grandmother might be able to work her culinary magic on him or, at least, offer some advice," she admitted.

The screen door squeaked and both turned to see Mark there. He motioned for them to come in.

"Looks like dinner is ready," Lucas said and the boy nodded.

"How's your family taking the news about Zebulon's involvement in the family line?" Thelma asked bluntly as they all sat down.

"Calmly," Lucas replied.

Thelma looked relieved. "I'm glad. Zebulon's a good man once you get past the prickly outer coating. Do you think your mother and grandmother might come for a visit?"

"I think they need a little more time to adjust before they make any decisions like that."

Thelma smiled warmly. "I can understand that."

Sensing Lucas's discomfort with this subject, Felicity said, "I noticed on your business card that you're a banker."

"My father's family has been in the banking business for several generations," he replied, then lifting a forkful of food, he added, "This is the best meal I've had in a long time."

Catching the hint that he'd rather eat than talk, Felicity simply raised her fork in a salute of agreement while her grandmother flushed with pleasure.

As the adults allowed a silence to fall over the table so that they could apply themselves to eating, Felicity covertly studied Mark. She knew there were women without maternal instincts but the boy was so cute she found it hard to believe he couldn't melt even the coldest heart.

As if he felt her eyes on him, he looked up at her questioningly. She grinned and winked and he winked back. A warm glow spread through her.

Noticing the exchange between Felicity and his son, Lucas was aware of her pleasure toward Mark's friendly response. He was beginning to sense a deep maternal instinct in the lawyer. The thought that he could be very wrong in limiting his choice of a wife to a stay-at-home mom grew stronger. He also found himself thinking that he should stick around Smytheshire for a little longer. His son obviously liked Felicity and he could not deny he was drawn to her as he'd never been drawn to a woman before.

Following the meal, all four pitched in to clean up. When Felicity lifted Mark so that he could put away a glass on a high shelf, he giggled. She'd never heard such a sweet sound. Setting him back on the floor, she couldn't believe how fond she'd grown of him in such a short time.

Suddenly the image of herself, Mark and Lucas as a family filled her mind. They were living in a large brick house. Mark was asleep in his room upstairs. She and Lucas were in the living room. A plush, cream-colored carpet covered the floor. The furniture was clearly expensive but very comfortable. There was a fireplace with a fire blazing. She and Lucas were curled up on a couch. He ran his hand along the curve of her body and flames as hot as those in front of her threatened to consume her.

"All done," Thelma announced cheerfully. "How about if we all go sit on the porch, enjoy the evening breeze and have a cool glass of lemonade."

A cool glass of anything poured right over my head would be a good idea, Felicity thought, abruptly pushing the image of her and Lucas from her mind.

Lucas jerked his gaze away from Felicity. He'd been having the most salacious daydream centering on the two of them. "A cold drink sounds like a good idea to me," he said.

Mark was already helping Thelma put ice in the glasses.

Determined not to allow herself to begin fantasizing about Lucas again, Felicity concentrated on the boy. "Do you play checkers?"

He turned to her and nodded shyly as if uncertain of his skill.

"How about a game?" she coaxed.

His eyes gleamed and he nodded again.

As Felicity set the checkerboard up on the table on the porch, she heard her grandmother politely but subtly probing into Lucas's background and marital status. Lucas, she noticed, answered honestly regarding his divorce but didn't elaborate. As for his family, he seemed perfectly comfortable talking about them. She sensed love there. But then, she'd known by the way he was with his son that he was a family-orientated man. He had a nice laugh, too, she thought when he laughed at an anecdote her grandmother told.

Glancing toward him, she discovered him looking her way. There was masculine interest in his eyes and a curl of excitement twisted through her. She wasn't ready to have these kinds of feelings again. She was never going to be ready to have them again. Ordering herself to ignore him, she once again turned her full concentration to Mark.

The boy was clever, she noted, having very little trouble making certain he won. They were finishing their second game when her thoughts drifted back to the house with the large fireplace. Again, she was there in Lucas's embrace. My imagination is really working overtime, she admonished herself and forcefully shoved the image out.

Lucas had managed, with a great deal of effort, to pay enough attention to the story Thelma was telling to get the gist of it. But it was Felicity who was constantly at the forefront of his mind. He again found himself picturing her in his home. She seemed to fit so perfectly there. An inner sense seemed to be suggesting that she was the missing piece he needed to make his life complete.

Mark yawned widely as he jumped Felicity's last checker.

Noticing Thelma yawn as well, Lucas glanced at his watch. It was later than he'd thought. The only polite thing to do would be to leave. "Looks like it's time Mark and I were on our way back to the inn," he said, rising from his chair. Besides, putting some distance between himself and Felicity might be a good idea, he reasoned. Thinking clearly in her presence was difficult and he needed to consider the effect she was having on him.

Regret spread over Mark's face.

"If you're staying in town for a while, come back and visit anytime," Thelma offered warmly.

Mark smiled widely while Lucas thanked her for the invitation.

Watching them drive away a few minutes later, Felicity experienced an intense rush of loneliness. Her jaw tensed in her effort to ignore it.

"Lucas Carver strikes me as very good husband material," Thelma said, waving a final goodbye to their departing guests.

Bile rose in Felicity's throat. "I tried that once. One failed marriage is enough for me."

Thelma frowned. "You simply married the wrong man."

"I have no confidence in being able to pick the right one. Therefore, I intend to remain single," Felicity replied firmly.

"I think you're passing up a very promising opportunity," Thelma warned.

"And I think it's time for bed," Felicity replied.

Thelma shook her head at her granddaughter's stubbornness and went inside.

Felicity quickly put the checker game in its box and followed. But as she climbed into bed a little later, Lucas's image again taunted her. "Better safe than sorry," she cautioned herself and shoved it out once again.

* * *

Back at the inn, Lucas tucked Mark into bed. His son had been unusually pensive, and he wondered what was on his mind.

"Is something bothering you, son?" he asked. It was a rhetorical question, he didn't really expect an answer. Still, he always conversed with Mark as if the boy might actually speak.

"Want Felicity for my mother."

Lucas blinked. Each word had been pronounced separately, sounding as if it were being twisted around Mark's tongue in his effort to pronounce it correctly. The effect was a slurred distortion but discernible. "You spoke." Euphoria filled Lucas. Laughing, he lifted his son out of bed and held him above his head then brought him down and gave him a hug.

As he stood Mark back on the bed, the boy looked hard into his father's face. "Want Felicity for my mother," he repeated.

Still in a state of semishock, Lucas did not want to take any chances on having misunderstood. "You want me to marry Felicity Burrow?"

Mark nodded furiously. "My mother...her."

Lucas grinned. All the way home Felicity had been on his mind. In spite of telling himself that he needed some distance between them to consider the effect she was having on him, he'd hated leaving her. As he'd driven away, he'd had the strangest sensation that he'd left something very important behind...something he needed to be complete. "It seems we're both on the same wavelength. We've each found something we don't want to live without and it's the same thing." Purpose showed on his face. "I'll see what I can do about it."

The boy grinned back, then yawned widely. "Sleep," he said.

Lucas laughed again from the sheer joy of hearing his son's voice. "Yes, sleep," he agreed and again tucked Mark in.

When the boy was settled comfortably, Lucas picked up the phone and dialed his parents' number. It was three hours earlier in Seattle but even if it had been three hours later, he would have called. He knew they would want to hear this news as quickly as possible.

His mother answered. "How is the trip going?" she asked.

He heard the hopefulness in her voice. "Very well," he replied. "Your grandson has spoken his first words."

There was a gasp on the other end of the line. Then Joline Carver asked shakily, "He spoke? He actually spoke?"

"He finally found something he didn't want to live without," Lucas replied.

"I'm so happy!"

In his mind's eye Lucas could see the tears of relief and joy streaming down his mother's face.

"What's happened?" he heard his father demanding in the background.

"Mark has spoken," Joline replied.

"Thank goodness," Ethan Carver's voice sounded in the distance. In the next instant, it was his voice coming over the line. "When are you coming home, son?"

"I need to stay for a while longer."

"Stay as long as is necessary. I can handle the business."

Lucas barely managed to say, "Thanks, Dad," before his mother was again on the line.

"What was it that Mark couldn't live without?" she asked.

No sense in hedging on this, Lucas decided. Mark was certain to tell her. "He's found someone he wants for his mother."

For a moment there was silence on the line, then Joline asked, "How do you feel about this woman?" Her voice became stern. "You can't marry her simply for Mark's sake. I thought you would have learned that by now."

Felicity's image was again at the forefront of Lucas's mind and a fire ignited within him. "Believe me, my interest in this woman is not simply because of Mark."

"You take time to be certain of that," his mother cautioned, not sounding totally convinced.

"Don't worry, Mom. I know what I'm doing," he assured her.

But later, lying in bed, Lucas frowned into the darkness. He had met Felicity Burrow just a little more than twenty-four hours ago. A conservative man who never rushed into anything without thought, it didn't seem reasonable he could be so certain she was the woman he wanted to marry. Still, he knew without a doubt she was.

Actually there was one other time when he'd acted on instinct, he reminded himself. That had been when he'd learned of his impending fatherhood and had wanted his child. His instincts had been correct then, and he trusted them now.

Felicity. He was certain she was attracted to him. He'd sensed it too strongly to be mistaken. Even more, he'd seen it in her eyes. But he'd also been aware she was fighting the attraction. Something about him made the lady nervous. He recalled his intent to find out why she was so uncomfortable in his presence and frowned impatiently at himself. He'd lost the opportunity and never found another.

She's probably just exercising an instinctual caution, he reasoned. Lawyers, it had been his experience, were a naturally wary breed.

A smile played at the corners of his mouth. He would start with flowers, he decided.

Felicity had been climbing into bed when a rush of euphoria swept through her. It was as if a tremendous weight had been lifted from her shoulders. Had her grandmother suddenly solved some problem that had been bothering her, she wondered? Or perhaps, Thelma had thought of a way to help Mark. Slipping her feet back into her slippers, she went down the hall and peeked in at her grandmother. Thelma was sleeping peacefully.

Returning to her room, Felicity realized the sensation had ceased. She felt normal once again. "Curious," she murmured. She'd never had an experience quite like that before.

Lucas Carver again entered her mind. She saw herself standing at an altar with him. They were being married. "No way! Not ever again," she vowed and pushed the vision from her mind.

Chapter Six

"We see Felicity?" Mark asked as he and his father prepared to go downstairs for breakfast the next morning.

"Yes, in a little while," Lucas promised. "However, I think it would be best if you simply say hello. We won't mention our intention of making her your mother just yet."

Mark frowned unhappily.

"Women like to be courted," Lucas explained.

Mark's expression turned to one of confusion.

"We have to give her time to learn to like us better . . . to let us be her best friends," Lucas elaborated.

"Are her friends," Mark insisted.

"You have to trust me to know what's best," Lucas coaxed. "Okay?"

For a moment longer Mark hesitated. Finally he nodded.

* * *

Pulling into the parking lot beside her office, Felicity saw Lucas and Mark sitting on the porch step. Silently she groaned. She was happy to see the child but she would rather the father had left town. Each time she saw him, her resolve was threatened. As she climbed out of the car, Mark ran down the walk toward her.

His face was filled with glee and she smiled warmly down at him. "Good morning."

"Hello," he responded, the word coming with a babyish slur.

Dropping her briefcase, Felicity squatted in front of him. "You spoke," she exclaimed with delight.

He nodded solemnly, his expression that of a person who had made the decision to follow a new path. Then his expression became even more solemn. "We friends?"

She noted that unlike herself when she'd first begun to speak, Mark pronounced his words separately as if each were its own sentence. They were not totally, correctly formed, but by him separating them, she could discern what he was saying. "Yes, of course," she replied, giving him a tight hug.

As she released him, he smiled shy. "Be my—"

"It would seem that you and your grandmother can work miracles." Lucas interrupted his son.

Suddenly looking worried that he'd done something wrong, Mark glanced up at his father. Lucas ruffled the child's hair and grinned down at him affectionately. But Felicity was certain that behind the love in his eyes, there was a warning.

"I owe you a debt of gratitude," Lucas continued, returning his full attention to Felicity as she straightened to a standing position. "Do you think we could impose upon your grandmother and ask her to baby-sit Mark while I take you out to dinner?''

"Not a baby," Mark interrupted curtly.

"I meant to say that we'll ask Thelma to keep my son company." Lucas restated his question.

Mark nodded his approval of this new phrasing, then looked hopefully at Felicity. "You eat with my daddy?" he asked.

Although she found it difficult to refuse the boy, Felicity had no intention of spending any time alone with Lucas. "I can't. I've got a lot of work to catch up on."

Lucas studied her thoughtfully. The first statement had carried the ring of conviction. The second had been a definite lie. A thought occurred to him. "Are you currently seeing someone?" he asked, determined that if the answer was yes, he would convince her that whoever she was involved with was wrong for her.

Felicity considered saying that she was seriously dating someone but she didn't like lying and she'd already done that enough this morning. "No. I'm simply very busy with my career at the moment."

"All work and no play makes for a very dull existence," he cautioned.

For a moment the thought that he could be a lot of fun played through her mind. Not again! she told herself curtly and pushed the thought aside. Rewarding his observation with a quick dry smile, she turned her attention to Mark. Squatting in front of the boy again, she said, "I'm so pleased you've decided to talk to us," then gave him a second hug. "Was it something my grandmother said?"

"Like you, he found something he wanted enough to speak up for it," Lucas replied before Mark had a chance to respond.

"You eat with my daddy?" Mark asked, his expression and tone begging her to reconsider.

Felicity's gaze traveled upward over Lucas's body as she straightened. A heat flared within her. Again her resolve was threatened. Again she reminded herself of the possible hurt. The desire to know exactly what had prompted the boy to begin talking was overpowered by a stronger desire to escape. She glanced at her watch, to give the impression of being on a tight schedule. "I've got to run. I've got an early appointment."

But before hurrying away, she could not resist pausing to kiss Mark on the top of the head. "Congratulations," she said, with loving warmth. Then without even looking at Lucas, she grabbed her briefcase and headed to her office.

Lucas watched her departure with a frown. He'd seen the heat in her eyes followed by the ice. And, the part about her needing to run had not been a lie but the bit about an appointment had. He was absolutely certain she was running away from him. But why?

Feeling Lucas's eyes on her, a curl of excitement traveled through Felicity. She forced herself to think of Jeff Lomax. A coldness descended over her and she continued inside feeling no regret at having refused the dinner invitation.

Lucas had the sudden very strong vision of a tall, slender, handsome black-haired man with brown eyes. Mark pulled on his hand and the image disappeared as he turned his attention to his son.

There was anxiousness on the boy's face. "Felicity not be my mother?"

"Don't worry. We're not going to give up so easily," Lucas assured him.

Mark smiled with relief.

"Maybe we should have started with flowers," Lucas said, as he pulled out of the parking lot. After all that had been his first plan. But when they'd passed the florist shop on their way to Felicity's office, it had been closed and he hadn't wanted to wait until it opened to see her.

Mark nodded. "Flowers."

"And I think I've come up with an invitation she can't refuse," Lucas added, a mischievous gleam in his eyes. "We'll need two bouquets. One we'll have delivered and the other we'll deliver ourselves."

An hour later, Lucas was turning onto the driveway leading to the Burrow home. Ahead, seated on the porch in her rocking chair was Thelma Burrow.

"Morning," he called as he climbed out of his car, then went around to open Mark's door.

"Morning," she called back, rising and coming off the porch to greet them. She was smiling warmly. "Felicity phoned to tell me Mark was talking."

Lucas returned her smile. "We came to thank you."

Mark held the newly purchased bouquet out to her. "Flowers."

She bent down to accept them and her smile warmed even more. "Thank you."

The boy grinned back, clearly pleased with the reception of his gift.

"Dinner was delicious," Lucas said, placing a hand under Thelma's elbow to help her straighten. "Mark and I would like to repay you by taking you and your granddaughter out tonight. I understand The Wainwright Inn serves excellent meals."

Thelma's eyes sparkled. "Marigold does a fine job in the kitchen."

"Then you'll join us?"

Thelma's grin broadened. "We'd love to. A night on the town with two handsome men is too much for me to pass up."

Lucas admitted he was being underhanded but he didn't care. All's fair in love and war, he reminded himself. "We'll pick you up at six-thirty."

As he began to usher Mark back to the car, Thelma laid a restraining hand on his arm. "I'm curious. Do you know why your son started talking?"

"He found something he couldn't live without."

The curiosity in her eyes increased. "And what was that?"

Mentally Lucas kicked himself. "Your chocolate cake."

"Felicity." Mark corrected him. "Want her for my mother."

For a moment Thelma stared at the boy in stunned silence while Lucas wished Mark had run all the words together rather than pronounce each with painful separateness. Even with the babyish slurring, he was easy to understand.

Mark glanced worriedly up at his father. Clearly Thelma's surprise had made him uneasy. "Should not told?" he asked anxiously.

Lucas forced a smile. What was done was done. He ruffled his son's hair. "It's all right."

"My granddaughter is an excellent choice," Thelma said, finding her voice. The smile on her face did not reach her eyes, though, when her gaze shifted to Lucas. Instead there was concern in those brown depths. "But I'd never advise anyone to marry simply on a child's preference."

"That would be a very foolish thing to do," he agreed.

"Very foolish," she repeated sternly.

Lucas's expression became solemnly serious. "For my own sake, I am interested in courting your grand-daughter. But I have the feeling that if she knew how Mark felt, she might not give me a chance. I'd appreciate it if you wouldn't mention my son's hope to Felicity."

Thelma regarded him in silence for a tense moment. "All right," she agreed finally. Her gaze leveled on him. "But I should warn you. My granddaughter has an uncanny knack for knowing when someone is lying."

"A very useful talent for a lawyer," Lucas replied.

Driving away, he frowned thoughtfully. His father had described his ability to read people in nearly the same terms Thelma Burrow had used to describe her granddaughter's knack. A curious coincidence or two minds that think along the same paths? he wondered. Either way, he was more certain than ever that Felicity Burrow was the perfect match for him. Just the thought of her caused his blood to heat.

Felicity sat staring at the bouquet of flowers that had arrived moments earlier. Lucas Carver didn't give up easily, she admitted. Her gaze shifted to the card in her hand. It read:

You have to eat. Since you won't have dinner with me alone, I've invited your grandmother. Mark will also accompany us. I've made reservations at the Wainwright Inn for seven. I'll pick you up at your home at 6:30.

Lucas

Felicity tapped the note on the desk in an impatient rapping beat. Lucas's image came into her mind and her blood suddenly warmed. Resolve etched itself into her features. He would be eating with her grandmother and Mark but not her!

Picking up the phone, she dialed her grandmother.

"I thought we'd stop by and see your great-great-grandfather again," Lucas said as he and Mark left the Burrow home. "We'll let him know we're staying on for a while. And, it does seem only right that we should get to know him a little better."

"Great...great...grandfather," Mark repeated with an approving nod.

"And Mutt," Lucas added.

Mark's eyes gleamed. "And Mutt."

Zebulon came out the front door to greet them as they parked. "Good to see you and your son again, lad," he said. "I was honest with you for the boy's sake, but I was afraid you might think I was too crazy for you to have anything more to do with me."

"I was skeptical. I still am," Lucas replied honestly.

Zebulon eyed him narrowly. "You going to take the boy by to see Celina?"

"I already did."

"Mutt!" Mark suddenly called out as the dog came around the house and into view.

Zebulon grinned. "Guess she was able to help." Watching the boy run to the dog, his grin turned to a frown. "Now that is peculiar. I've never known her to actually cure anyone of anything."

"Celina didn't cure him."

Zebulon swung his attention back to Lucas. "How'd he start talking then?"

Lucas studied the old man closely. "It was Felicity."

Zebulon's grin returned and he nodded. "I remembered that girl hadn't talked right off. But I never knew what popped her cork and got the words flowing."

"That's why you brought her with you that first night you came to see me, isn't it?" Lucas challenged.

Zebulon nodded. "Thought she might take pity on the boy and tell you what had made her talk. Besides, I needed someone to drive me. Gave that up a while back." Interest gleamed in the old man's eyes. "You going to tell me what loosened his tongue?"

"Like her, he found something he didn't want to live without."

"And what might that be?" Zebulon coaxed.

"I need your word, you won't tell," Lucas bargained.

"You've got it."

"He wants Felicity Burrow for his mother," Lucas said bluntly.

Zebulon nodded with approval. "A man could do worse." A sudden cautioning entered his voice. "But if you do go courting her, don't ever try to lie to her. That girl's real sharp about things like that. She can spot a tall tale a mile away. That's another reason I brought her along the other night."

It would seem that he and Felicity very definitely had a great deal in common, Lucas mused.

"Do you have time to sit a spell?" Zebulon motioned toward the chairs on the porch.

Lucas noted that Mark was already playing with Mutt in the shade of the huge old oak. "Yes. I'd like to hear more about you and the rest of the Lanskys."

"T'ain't much to tell," Zebulon said as he stepped up onto the porch then eased himself into a rocking chair.

"We're just plain folks. My daddy and his daddy farmed the land, raised cattle, fished and hunted to put food on the table. But farming weren't for me. I traveled for a while."

A glaze of reminiscence came over his eyes. "That's when I met your great-grandmother."

He gave his shoulders a shake as if they felt too burdened with memories and he wanted to rid himself of some. "Came back here soon after that. I'd had my fill of traveling. Farmed with my father and grandfather until they died. But, like I just said, it weren't the life for me. We'd always left this land around the lake in its wild state. Oh, periodically, we'd hire a few loggers to harvest some of the trees for a bit of extra cash but we never let them take so much it hurt the natural beauty of the place. After they died, I started letting more land go back to the wild. Finally sold off the more usable acreage and settled in up here."

"You never married?"

Again the reminiscent haze came over Zebulon's eyes. "Never met anyone who could turn my head like Linette." Again he gave his shoulders a shake, then picked up a piece of wood lying near his chair. It was beginning to resemble a bird. Taking out his pocketknife, he started giving more definition to the fowl. "Tell me about her. Did she have a good life? And your grandmother, my daughter..." his tongue seemed to linger on these last words as if getting used to the feel of them. "Tell me about her and your mother. Are they happy?"

"Yes," Lucas replied. Unexpectedly an uneasiness washed over him and in his mind's eye he saw Felicity scowling at a bouquet of flowers. As quickly as it had come, the vision was gone but the concern that she would reject his invitation lingered. No sense in worrying before I know there's something to worry about, he told himself. Returning his full attention to Zebulon, he began telling stories he thought the old man would enjoy hearing.

"Felicity won't be joining us," Thelma said apologetically when Lucas and Mark arrived to escort the women to dinner. "She's still at her office. A new client came in this afternoon."

Lucas sensed doubt behind Thelma's words as if she wasn't so sure her granddaughter's excuse was true. He had a strong notion it wasn't. Taking Thelma by the arm to help her off the porch, he forced a smile. "Well, at least we'll have the pleasure of the company of one of the very charming Burrow women."

Mark continued to stare at the house, clearly waiting for Felicity to appear.

"Come on, son," Lucas coaxed, taking Mark's hand in his free one.

The smile that had been on Mark's face when they arrived was now gone. He said nothing, but Lucas could feel the boy's sense of rejection like a physical blow. Maybe, for his son's sake, pursuing Felicity Burrow was a mistake. He'd been so determined that he would win her, he hadn't thought about the effects of failure. His son did not need to be spurned again.

As they reached the car, Thelma smiled encouragingly at Mark. "I hope you don't mind having dinner with just me."

The boy reached up and touched her arm in a gentle caress and smiled back. But Lucas noticed the lingering sadness in Mark's eyes. Even more, he realized his son had not spoken but had reverted to sign language once again.

* * *

Felicity sat at her desk, trying to concentrate on the will in front of her when a sharp jab of rejection cut through her like a knife. The sensation was so intense, tears filled her eyes.

She glanced toward the door of her office. Peggy had gone home over an hour ago. Had her secretary left the front door unlocked and a new client walked in? she wondered. If so, the person was in great agony over his or her problem. She hadn't heard anyone enter but then her mind had been elsewhere.

Rising from her desk, she went into the outer office. No one was there, and the door was bolted. She glanced at her watch. It was just past six-thirty. The image of a dejected little boy flashed into her mind and she knew without a doubt that the sudden hurt she'd experienced had come from Mark.

There were other young children in her life...children of cousins and friends. She was fond of them very fond of some. But she'd never experienced this kind of connection to any of them. Normally she had to be in their presence to sense their feelings and even then, the sensation was not this strong. Her heart refused to allow Mark to think she did not like him.

With no further thought than to ease the child's pain, she grabbed her purse, turned off the lights and left her office. She was sitting in one of the rocking chairs on the porch of the Wainwright Inn when Lucas pulled into the parking lot.

Lucas nearly clipped the fender of a red Mustang. He blinked once just to be certain he wasn't seeing things. He wasn't. Felicity was there. He'd been picturing her waiting for them, but he hadn't really expected her to be there.

Thelma grinned with approval. "It would seem that Felicity has decided to join us after all."

Lucas glanced toward his son to see Mark smiling widely. Just in case Miss Felicity Burrow refused to be courted, he was going to have to find a way to ease his son's disappointment.

"Evening," Felicity said, leaving the porch to meet the trio as they climbed out of the car. She glanced briefly at her grandmother and Lucas, then turned her full attention to Mark. "I could not miss this celebration dinner. I'm so proud of you," she said, holding out her hand to him.

Continuing to hold on to his father with one hand, he took hers as well. "Daddy. Mommy," he said happily.

Felicity again pictured the three of them as a family. Clearly that was what Mark wanted and for one brief second she did, too. Then reality clicked in. No! she rebelled silently. Coming to an abrupt halt, she squatted in front of the boy. "I want very much to be your *friend.*"

He grinned and touched her face lovingly. "Friend. Mommy."

Deciding this was neither the time nor the place for a discussion of his wishes, Felicity kissed him lightly on the nose, then straightened.

As they continued on to the entrance of the inn, she glanced at Lucas. His expression was polite, but she knew it was a mask. She sensed an uneasiness. A part of him seemed glad to see her while another part was withdrawn. She surmised that he was hiding his embarrassment at his son's forwardness. Obviously he was not as sure as Mark was that they'd make a great family.

And that's good, she declared. Maybe he would keep his distance and she could relax.

Reaching the porch, Lucas released his son and quickly opened the door. He hoped Mark would be discreet. But what was done was done.

Thelma entered first. Mark followed with Felicity in tow. Unexpectedly the image of Lucas laying his hand on her shoulder, then moving it caressingly to her neck entered Felicity's mind as she passed him. It was so real, she glanced back. Lucas was merely holding the door politely for her. But as she continued into the inn, the image came back even more strongly. His hands were on her waist now and slowly they moved downward as he proceeded with his exploration along the line of her hips. An erotic smoldering heat spread through her.

She'd always been able to sense when a man was interested in her but her imagination had never taken over and added arousing imagery. Maybe she'd been wrong to isolate herself so completely from male companionship. Clearly her hormones were not ready to accept her vow never to become romantically involved again. Well, they're going to have to! she insisted and shoved the uninvited imagery from her mind.

Sitting down at their table, Lucas forced himself to concentrate, first on the menu and then on his son and Thelma. Whenever his attention turned to Felicity, he could not stop himself from wondering how her lips would taste or her neck or perhaps her shoulder. Then his mind would want to wander to more intimate areas. He would find himself so engrossed in thoughts of her, all else would be blanked out. When he'd followed her inside, his gaze had been captured so completely by the curve of her hips, he'd nearly tripped over the threshold.

Maybe what he felt for her was purely lust, he cautioned himself. But if it was, it was the strongest case he'd ever had or even heard about. However, not wanting to look like a drooling idiot, he kept his attention off her as much as possible during the meal.

Felicity was agitated as she drove home. Lucas had blatantly ignored her all during dinner. She hadn't wanted his attention, but she also hadn't enjoyed being made to feel like an unwelcome nuisance. Obviously his son's desire to have her for a mother had put a damper on Lucas's interest. The man might have been looking for a playmate but not a wife.

"Well, you've certainly managed to put Lucas Carver off," Thelma said, letting Felicity know that she, too, had noticed Lucas's behavior. "Guess he won't be coming by again."

"That suits me just fine," Felicity returned. "Obviously his interest in me was a fleeting fancy." Mentally she congratulated herself for keeping her vow to steer clear of romantic entanglements.

"He did seem to give up easily." Thelma shook her head. "I'd never have guessed he was such a shallow man."

"You can't judge a book by its cover."

"Apparently not," Thelma conceded.

"I need to go out for a while, son," Lucas said as he tucked Mark into bed. He nodded toward Betty Truesdale, seated in a rocking chair in the far corner of the room, knitting quietly. "Mrs. Truesdale will be right here if you need anything."

Mark smiled at the pleasant-faced proprietress and she smiled back.

As he left the Apple Tree Inn, Lucas's instincts assured him his son would be safe. They also warned him that he had damage to undo where the Burrow women was concerned. Wanting to protect his son from further disappointment, when Felicity had said she was finished at her office for the day and would drive her grandmother home, he had not insisted on escorting the ladies to their door.

"I should be getting Mark back to the inn and into bed," he'd said instead.

From Thelma he'd sensed disillusionment. Clearly she felt she'd misjudged him and was unhappy with herself for being deceived. From Felicity there had been an "I knew it" look in her eyes that said he'd lived down to her expectations.

"Time to mend some fences," he muttered as he drove out of town.

Felicity sat on the porch with her grandmother. When they'd returned home from dinner, she'd intended to go to bed and curl up with a good book but the restlessness she'd been experiencing the past few days had returned full force. Preferring company to being alone, she'd joined her grandmother.

"Your grandpa used to call that a lover's moon," Thelma said, her gaze resting on the sliver of silver in the night sky. "He'd say it was just bright enough to light the way to my door but not so bright we couldn't have our privacy."

Felicity smiled. "I never thought of grandpa as being so romantic."

"He had his moments."

Felicity felt a nudge of envy and her restlessness increased.

The sound of a car interrupted the stillness of the night. "I wonder who that could be?" Thelma peered at the road. A frown creased her brow when the car slowed, then turned into their driveway. "Looks like Lucas."

Felicity scowled. "What could he want?" As the car came to a stop and the engine was shut off, she rose. "I'm sure that whatever he's come for involves you and not me. I'm going inside."

"Felicity, you can't keep running away from me forever," Lucas called out, quickly climbing out of the car and striding toward the porch.

She paused with her hand on the door and turned back to regard him haughtily. "I was under the impression that you preferred not to speak to me."

"You were standoffish toward my granddaughter all during dinner," Thelma confirmed, watching him suspiciously. "Never could abide a man who blew hot or cold depending on his mood."

Lucas leveled his gaze on her. "My son has chosen your granddaughter for his mother. He's been rejected by his biological mother, and I don't want him going through a similar experience once again. So I figured I should have a private talk with Felicity before I pursued her any further."

Felicity glared at him. "I am not interested in being pursued by you or any man, and I most certainly would not consider marrying a man merely for the sake of his son. As I told Mark, I want to be his friend but I will go no further."

Lucas turned to her. "If we marry, it will not be only for my son's sake."

The heat in his eyes caused her blood to race. Her jaw tensed. She'd played the fool once but never again. "I find your renewed show of interest in me a little hard to believe. You had no trouble ignoring me all during dinner."

"You're wrong. I had a very hard time ignoring you during dinner."

Her scowl deepened. "You admit you were trying to ignore me?"

The heat in his eyes grew more intense. "I have always been in control of my emotions. Even as a teenager, I never let them rule my judgment. But every time I look at you, I have the most lecherous thoughts."

Felicity found herself picturing him nibbling on her earlobe and her blood again threatened to race. "I'm really not interested," she said stiffly.

"Yes, you are," he called her bluff. "What I don't know is why you're fighting so hard not to be. It isn't because of Mark. You're genuinely fond of my son. As for myself, I'm respectable, honest, hardworking. I can support you in a comfortable life-style."

"I'm simply not interested in marriage...been there, done it, don't want to do it again," she said succinctly.

Lucas's hand closed around her arm, stopping her when she started to enter the house. "You've been married?"

"It's a part of my life I'd rather forget." She attempted to pull free.

Lucas's hold tightened. "Everyone makes mistakes. That's part of life."

"I've been telling her that same thing for the past four years." Thelma eased herself out of her rocking chair. "Maybe you can talk some sense into her. It's time for me to go inside and leave the two of you alone."

"I have no intention of staying out here," Felicity insisted, again trying to jerk free.

"If you'll quit wiggling I'll let go," Lucas bargained. "But I'm not leaving until we talk this out."

"There is nothing to 'talk out,'" Felicity insisted.

"You just sit yourself down and talk to the man," Thelma ordered, pointing to the chair she'd recently occupied. "Seems to me he's a fine catch. I don't see any reason for you tossing him back without taking a longer look."

Felicity started to argue with her grandmother, but the set of Thelma's jaw let her know protesting would be useless. As Lucas released her, she issued a disgruntled snort and moved away from the door to allow her grandmother to enter the house. Seating herself in the rocking chair, she noticed that the heat of his hand continued to linger on her skin. Even worse, it was stirring embers to life within. She glowered up at him. "You're right. People do make mistakes, but I have no intention of making the same one twice."

"What makes you so certain I would be a mistake?" he challenged.

"I'm not certain. I simply don't want to take the chance."

"Clearly you took a chance once."

"I didn't think it was a chance. I thought it was a sure thing."

"There are very few sure things in this life."

"So I learned."

Her resolve, Lucas noted, was the strongest he'd ever sensed in anyone. But he was determined to find a chink in her armor. "What happened?"

"I trusted my instincts. I didn't realize there was a serious flaw in the way they worked until it was too late." Felicity frowned at herself. She had never admitted her ability to rely on her intuition to anyone but her grandmother. Now she'd practically blurted it to a stranger.

Lucas sensed her withdrawal. "Your grandmother warned me that you would know if I lied. I have that same knack myself," he confessed, hoping this revelation would weaken the barrier she was again building around herself.

For a moment she stared at him in stunned silence. He certainly believed what he said. "You do?"

"I used to think I was simply more observant than other people. Now I'm not so sure that's the total answer," he confessed.

Felicity regarded him thoughtfully. "I've always assumed my knack was due to a heightened womanly intuition. Now, I guess I'll have to recategorize it into merely intuition." A cynical smile curled her lips. "The problem with this bit of intuitive ability is that what is the truth one moment might not be the truth the next."

"And that's the flaw?" he prompted when she fell silent.

She nodded. "People change. Or, more correctly, their emotions come in layers, one masking the other."

He sensed a bitterness deep within her. "Tell me what happened," he coaxed. "If I'm to be held accountable for another man's actions, I should, in all fairness, at least know what they were."

She scowled at him. "I'm not holding you accountable."

"You're refusing to give me a chance because of whatever your ex-husband did." He seated himself in a nearby chair. Putting his feet up on the railing, he crossed them at the ankles. Looking like a man who planned to stay indefinitely, he said, "I've got a couple more hours before I need to be back at the inn. That should be long enough for you to tell what I'm up against."

"You're definitely cut from the same cloth as Zebulon," she grumbled, sensing an unshakable resolve in him. "Both of you are as bullheaded as the day is long."

He grinned at her, a mischievous twinkle in his eyes. "I'll take that as a compliment."

Her heart skipped a beat. He was a serious threat to her resolve. She had to get rid of him. Besides, recalling the painful memories of her disastrous marriage was sure to keep her heart in line. "I met Jeff Lomax my first year in law school. He was a year ahead of me. Handsome, tall, black haired, brown eyed."

Lucas recalled the image that had flashed into his mind earlier in the day. Just a coincidence, he reasoned. He'd never received visual images from anyone before. Pushing the memory aside, he concentrated on what Felicity was saying.

"We dated only a short time. He was so intense. I could feel his wanting to protect me and care for me as if it was a warm soft blanket wrapped securely around me." She frowned up at the night sky. "I was nervous, uncertain about myself…immature in a lot of ways. He made me feel good about myself and secure in my future. I guess you could say I fell head over heels in love with him. We eloped during the winter break. It was very romantic."

Lucas sensed a strong jab of pain mingled with self-directed anger. "And then?" he urged.

A coldness crept through her. "The first months were wonderful. He was my mentor, my lover, my friend. And that summer was idyllic. The trouble began toward the end of the next term. I'd always been a good student and my grades were better than his had been in the same courses. I began to sense a change in him. I knew he didn't like my besting him, so I found myself making excuses as to why I was doing better than he had. I said the professor was obviously being more lenient with me because I was a woman. We both knew this was lie. If anything, the opposite was true."

Lucas scowled darkly. "He should have been happy for you."

"Yes, he should have been." Her jaw firmed. "But he wasn't. I could feel him growing more and more distant. I'm aware that people who love each other go through times when they're hurt or angry and their love is buried beneath those emotions for a while. But it's still there and comes back quickly. I hoped this was the case. We were both under a lot of pressure and stress. We went away for a second honeymoon to celebrate our first wedding anniversary."

She glanced up at what her grandmother had called a lover's moon as she recalled what was to have been a fairy-tale vacation but had been more of a nightmare. "I'd hoped we could recapture our love but he seemed impatient, restless all the time we were gone. When we got back to campus, I learned why. I'd been fighting my instincts. I stopped. He'd been tutoring a new freshman. I began to ask questions about her. I sensed an interest on his part that was more than a normal teacher-student emotion. When I asked him point-blank about his feeling toward her, he said they were merely professional, but I knew he was lying. I felt like a failure, like

I'd done something wrong. I tried being more romantic, catering to him more. I even found myself hiding my
test scores for fear they would upset him."

Lucas studied her. The self-directed anger he was
sensing was growing stronger as if she were mentally
calling herself a fool.

"It actually worked. But my behavior, constantly
apologizing for my success and hiding it when I could,
began to wear on my nerves. I found myself disliking
me. Then one day, he came home and announced he
had to have a divorce. His 'student' was pregnant with
his child. She was scared and needed him more than I
did. The warm blanket of love and security I'd once
sensed from him was entirely gone. In its place was only
indifference. I felt betrayed and humiliated but not so
much by Jeff as by myself. I'd tried to be someone I
wasn't to please him."

"I find it hard to believe you would worry about
making that mistake twice," Lucas said, noting the
hard, determined line of her jaw. "You're very definitely your own person."

"No. That mistake I would never make again. What
I don't know is how to tell lasting love from something
that is a fleeting whim of the moment." Her gaze leveled on him. "Jeff did love me. But only while I ful-
filled his need to be my mentor and protector. When I
became strong enough to be my own person, he lost interest. I gave him the divorce without hesitation. Any
tender feelings I had toward him were gone. I took back
my maiden name. I wanted no reminders of what a fool
I'd been."

Again Lucas sensed extreme self-directed anger.

"Afterward, a woman by the name of Sheree Val-
deze approached me. I knew who she was. We'd never

had any real contact but once she'd been at a party Jeff and I'd attended. I'd noticed her watching me from across the room. There had been a cynical look on her face. One of the women standing near me had noticed also and told me that Sheree had been Jeff's girlfriend his first year in law school. Anyway, this Sheree had come by to offer sympathy. I wasn't interested but she insisted she had something to tell me that I should know. She said she knew how I felt but that I shouldn't feel like a fool. When she'd first met Jeff, she'd been insecure. But as she'd proved to herself that she could succeed... when her grades came in and she made the Dean's list... she'd become more assertive, more sure of herself and he'd lost interest. He'd dumped her and found a new girlfriend, another lost lamb type. The same scenario had played out again. When his new girlfriend had become more confident in herself he'd dumped her."

Felicity's frown deepened. "He'd had an affair with Sheree and the other girl. I'd never been the affair type, that's why he'd married me."

"What happened to the pregnant woman?" Lucas asked.

"He married her. She quit school and devoted herself to being a wife and mother. They seemed very happy together the last time I heard. And as long as she remains the adoring wife, basking in his shadow, I'm sure they'll be fine." She shrugged. "To each his own. I'm glad they both found happiness."

Lucas knew she was telling the truth. "I am not like Jeff Lomax. Confident women do not scare me. I admire them."

Felicity's gaze narrowed on him. "No, you're not Jeff Lomax. But you have a son you love deeply, and he wants me for his mother."

"I would not court a woman simply for my son's sake."

Challenge glowed in her eyes. "How can you be so certain of that? Jeff honestly believed he was in love with me . . . he believed he was in love with each of the women he became involved with." Without allowing him time to answer, she rose. "Good night and goodbye, Mr. Carver."

Lucas was on his feet in an instant. He caught her by the arm. "This isn't over, Felicity."

"Yes, it is." Jerking free, she went inside.

For a long moment Lucas stared at the door she'd closed between them, then stepped off the porch and headed to his car. At least he knew what he was up against. The problem was Mark. Lucas was not so vain he was certain he would win this struggle of wills and he didn't want his son hurt. He would have to convince Mark that having Felicity as a friend was as important and as good as having her for a mother. Besides, being her friend first was the best way to earn her trust, and he knew that until she trusted him, she would never allow herself to love him.

Chapter Seven

Felicity felt like purring. A strong male hand was gently stroking her back. She turned into a pair of powerful arms. Her cheek brushed against a hair-roughened chest. She looked upward. Lucas Carver smiled down at her, then his lips found hers. Desire raged like an uncontrolled fire within her. She moved closer to him and realized they were both naked.

Caressingly, his hands followed the curves of her body and she smiled with delight. Her breathing became ragged. He was kissing her shoulder now, and she raked her fingernails seductively over his back. When he groaned with satisfaction, a womanly power filled her. "Lucas," she breathed his name aloud.

The sound of her voice jarred her. Abruptly her eyes popped open. She was alone in her room, her arms wrapped around a pillow. Startled and shaken, she tossed the pillow to the floor as if getting rid of it would rid her of lingering sensations still tormenting her body.

But her blood continued to race and her heart to pound wildly. Even worse was the ache of loneliness and the wanting to be held in those strong male arms. Sitting up, she took several deep calming breaths.

"It was just a dream," she told herself, hoping the sound of her voice would help restore her to a more normal state. But the feeling of a need left unfulfilled continued to haunt her. She raked her hands through her hair. Never had a dream felt so real.

Lying back down, she ordered herself not to think of Lucas Carver. But when she closed her eyes, she saw a man's image reflected in a mirror. It was him sitting alone in a bed, the covers twisted and askew. He combed his hands through his hair, and she read confusion on his face as if he'd just woken and wasn't quite sure where he was. The urge to join him on his bed once again was strong.

She shoved the image from her mind. Contemplating legal precedents for a problem one of her clients had called about, she drifted back to sleep.

Lucas stared at his image in the mirror. He'd left the bathroom light on for Mark and the room was illuminated enough for him to see the look of consternation on his face.

He'd been having the most incredibly erotic dream about Miss Felicity Burrow. It had ended so abruptly he'd been jarred awake. He finished raking his hair away from his face with his fingers then rubbed the back of his neck. Never had a dream felt so real. He was still dazed. And extremely frustrated, he added suppressing a groan of discontent so as not to awaken his son.

That woman had one powerful hold on his imagination, he mused as he lay back down.

Felicity awoke the next morning feeling disconcerted and unfulfilled. She'd forgotten just how strong lust could be, she admitted as she drove to work. Lucas Carver's image tormented her. What made it worse was that she kept seeing him in various stages of undress. The temptation to spend some time with him nagged at her.

Her jaw hardened with resolve. There was no way she could be certain he was not courting her for his son's sake. He had not believed he was lying when he vowed that wasn't the case but he could be fooling himself. He loved his son deeply. That love coupled with the guilt he felt about the boy's mother not wanting her son could easily cause him to believe he was in love with her simply to give Mark what the boy most wanted. One bad marriage was enough for her.

Pulling into the parking lot beside her office, she groaned. This morning was going from bad to worse. Jerome Sayer's yellow pickup truck was parked beside her secretary's blue coupe and the sixty-two-year-old surly farmer was sitting inside. As she parked, he climbed out and approached her. Why had he sought her out? she wondered. When he needed a lawyer, he used one in Griswoldville. And that suited her just fine. She'd never liked him.

Jerome Sayer was much too self-righteous. Even more, as her grandmother put it, the man was just plain mean-spirited. He'd cast his daughter Emily out when she was sixteen and pregnant, leaving her to fend for herself and her unborn child on her own. Luckily, others in town were more softhearted. Felicity also suspected he'd beaten all of his children. She was two years younger than Patrick, his youngest son, and she could still remember the boy coming to school with bruises he'd said he'd gotten falling. She'd known he was lying.

With an effort she was able to keep her expression neutral as Jerome Sayer came to a halt in front of her. "Mr. Sayer," she said, extending her hand. She would rather have touched a snake, but she was determined to be polite.

He merely grunted acknowledgment of her greeting and, shoving his hands into the pockets of his overalls, refused her handshake. "There's rumors around town that this Lucas Carver is a long lost relative of Zebulon's. Doc's been saying as how he's the spitting image of an old photo he once saw and some of the old crones in town claim he looks like Zebulon as a young man."

Felicity's manner became that of the professional lawyer she was. "You will have to ask Zebulon about that."

"Wouldn't ask that crazy old man for the time of day," Jerome snarled.

"Then it would seem we don't have anything to talk about." Glad to be rid of the man's company, Felicity started toward her office.

"Not so fast, missy." Jerome caught her by the arm and jerked her back around hard.

The man was strong and she sensed intense rage. Fear swept through her, but she hid it well. "Let go of me or I'll file a complaint," she threatened.

Releasing her, he rubbed his hand on his overalls as if he'd just touched something distasteful. Then glowering down at her, he said, "Zebulon's grandma was a Sayer. My granddaddy's been keeping track of family ties. T'ain't none closer to Zebulon than us. If this stranger is a Lansky, he's a bastard and bastards ain't got no rights. That land of Zebulon's is Sayer land. He sold off most of what were originally Lansky holdings. The majority of what he's sitting on today was inherited by his grandma and rightly belongs to me and mine when the old man dies.''

Felicity met his gaze evenly. ''Zebulon's grandma inherited it from her mother's side of her family. That land was never Sayer land.''

''She were born a Sayer. That makes her land Sayer land.''

''Who the land once belonged to is not relevant. It belongs to Zebulon to do with as he pleases,'' Felicity said coolly.

''We Sayers ain't going to stand by and be robbed of what is rightfully ours. If'n he tries to will that land to anyone who ain't legal blood, we'll take the will to court.'' He stuck his face closer to hers. ''And I ain't talking just about this Carver character. I'm including you and your kin or Colin Darnell or anyone else hereabouts the old man takes a fancy to leaving something to. We'll claim undo influence on a demented old man.''

Felicity didn't think she'd ever felt such hate from anyone before. Fearful Jerome might actually try to strike her, she took a step back. ''Zebulon is in full control of his mental faculties.''

He sneered at her. ''You just better make sure that old coot does what's right.''

To Felicity's relief she heard a car pulling in. Glancing over her shoulder she saw it was Chief Brant. ''Everything all right here?'' he asked, parking and climbing out of the patrol car.

"Just fine," Jerome snarled. Giving Felicity one final warning glance, he then stalked back to his truck, climbed in and drove off.

"Peggy called me," Thatcher said as he and Felicity watched the yellow truck moving down the road. "She said he looked as if he might cause trouble."

Felicity glanced toward her offices to see her secretary standing on the porch. Smiling gratefully, she waved to let Peggy know everything was all right. The secretary waved back, then went inside and Felicity returned her attention to the lawman. "I don't like him. He scares me."

Thatcher turned to her. "Did he threaten you?"

"Not exactly. He's worried about Zebulon leaving his land to Lucas Carver. He claims it's Sayer land."

"Doc went to see Zebulon yesterday. The old man told him that Carver's a distant relative on the Lansky side."

Felicity heard the question in Thatcher's voice. "He is," she confirmed.

Thatcher nodded, letting her know he accepted her word on this. "You take care," he said and strode back to his patrol car.

Continuing into her office, she found Peggy hanging up the phone. "Thanks for calling the chief," she said. "I don't think Mr. Sayer would have harmed me, but he was getting pretty worked up."

Peggy shuddered. "He scares me."

"Me, too," Felicity admitted.

Peggy suddenly smiled. "I just made a 9:15 appointment for you. That fills your morning."

Accepting the slip of paper Peggy was handing her, Felicity glanced at the name. Lucas Carver, 9:15 was written in a precise hand. This morning was definitely turning into a challenge.

Trying not to think about Lucas, her mind returned to Jerome as she entered her office and seated herself at her desk. Clearly the man had given Zebulon's will a great deal of thought. He'd even managed to guess who the benefactors would be. Felicity had once thought that Zebulon might leave his land to an environmental group that would keep it as it was. But he loved it too much to leave it to strangers so, at the moment, his estate was to go half to her grandmother and half to Colin Darnell. Those two were the closest to friends the old man had. "And I'd like to see the Sayers try to break any will my grandfather drew up," she said with pride. "Or any will I might draw up," she added.

A sudden curl of expectation ran along her spine. Glancing to her window she saw Lucas approaching. He was carrying a vase filled with a huge bouquet of red roses and baby's breath. A surge of heat raced through her. The man seemed to get better looking with each passing day, she thought, then scowled at herself. He was seeking a mother for his son. That was the truth behind any feelings he had for her.

"Good morning," he said, as he entered.

"Good is not an adjective I would use to describe it so far," she returned dryly, rising but remaining behind her desk, keeping the wooden barrier between them. With her arms folded in front of her and a stern expression on her face, she watched him place the flowers on an uncluttered spot in front of her.

He frowned at the strength of her resistance. "You're a stubborn woman, Felicity Burrow."

"I thought we'd already established that." For one brief moment she felt a jolt of impatience from him, then it was gone. In its place was a sense of purpose.

"I have come here this morning to ask you to be a friend to my son."

Her frown softened at the thought of the young boy. "I am his friend." She glanced to the door of her office. "Why don't you ask him to join us so I can assure him of that myself?"

"He's not with your secretary. He's playing with Betty Truesdale's grandchildren. I wanted to have this talk with you alone." His expression grew grim. "Mark needs to feel secure in the knowledge that you are his friend. Simply telling him you are is not enough. He began talking because of you. When he thought you were not going to join us for dinner last night, he again withdrew. I would like for you to spend enough time with us for him to know you truly like him. I will promise to behave like a gentleman. However, that doesn't mean I won't try to change your mind about me."

Now certain she'd been right in her assessment of his motives, Felicity smiled confidently. "I will be happy to spend time with Mark. But you will be wasting your time and energy if you think you can convince me to fall in love with you."

He read her cynicism and his gaze narrowed on her. "I want you to be my son's friend for his sake. I want to marry you for mine."

Every instinct told her he was being honest. Again her early-morning dream filled her mind and she wondered what actually being in his arms would be like. Don't play the fool again, she admonished herself. Jeff had believed he was in love with her, too. She would not fall into that trap a second time. "I will not marry you, Mr. Carver," she stated firmly.

Lucas knew the wall between them was even stronger now than before and he wished he could have courted her without mentioning Mark. But he had to make certain his son would not be hurt. Images from his rude awakening in the early hours of the morning suddenly filled his mind. "A man can dream," he said.

Felicity saw the desire flame to life in his eyes and for one brief instant she again envisioned herself and Lucas as lovers wrapped in each other's arms.

Lucas forced the remembered images of himself and Felicity from his mind. They were too strong and the urge to take her in his arms was close to overwhelming. Fear that if he gave in to this impulse, she might not continue to agree to spend time with Mark was all that held him back.

Felicity drew a shaky breath as the images vanished. That dream should never have happened, and it's not going to happen again, she told herself firmly. She glanced at her watch. "I have another appointment in just a couple of minutes," she said with dismissal.

"Zebulon has invited us to go fishing this afternoon. What we catch, we'll fry for dinner. Will you join us?" he asked.

She wanted to say no but she could not turn away from Mark. "I'll meet you there."

"Six o'clock?"

"Six," she confirmed.

"Dress will be casual...jeans."

She nodded. "Jeans it is."

As he started to go, she recalled her encounter with Jerome Sayer. "Wait."

A jab of fear similar to the one he'd experienced earlier this morning, pierced Lucas. He'd been puzzled by the first one. There had been no reason for it. Now as he turned back to her, he suddenly wondered if it had come from her as well. If so... he shoved this possibility to the back of his mind for later consideration. "What's wrong?" he demanded.

That he'd sensed her apprehension so sharply surprised her. "I'm not sure anything is really wrong," she replied. "It's just that if I were you, I'd stay away from a man by the name of Jerome Sayer. He's a farmer in his early sixties, with a thick head of white hair, wears overalls and boots most of the time, heavyset, around five feet eleven inches, always has a snarl on his face and the meanest eyes you'll ever see."

Lucas regarded her questioningly. "Why should he concern me?"

"He thinks he and his family have a legitimate claim to Zebulon's land. He's worried Zebulon might rewrite his will and leave the land to you," she said bluntly.

Lucas frowned. "I didn't come here seeking anything but information from Zebulon."

"I know that."

Lucas continued to frown. "Does this Sayer person have a legitimate claim to Zebulon's land?"

Felicity shook her head. "Not by my reckoning. The Sayers haven't spoken to the Lanskys in two generations. Zebulon's grandmother married against her parents' wishes and when her mother's parents left all of their worldly possessions to her, which included the majority of what is now Zebulon's land, the Sayers considered that adding insult to injury."

Lucas nodded to indicate he agreed with her assessment. "I'll steer clear of anyone fitting Sayer's description." A sudden thought occurred to him and he smiled. "I appreciate your concern."

Her jaw tensed. "I'd be concerned about anyone Jerome Sayer took a particular dislike to."

Lucas suddenly approached her and traced the taut line of her jaw with his fingertip. "Come on, admit you do care a little for me."

Currents of heat raced through her. She took a step back out of his reach. "I'll admit I'm attracted to you, but lust isn't love, and I'm not giving in to either."

He'd seen the flash of desire in her eyes and the urge to remain and attempt to break through the barrier she kept so securely around herself was strong. Don't rush, he ordered himself. "Six," he said, reminding her of her agreement to eat with him, Zebulon and Mark, then he quickly left.

Startled by his abrupt departure, Felicity stood frozen staring at the door. Then her gaze shifted to the window and she watched him walking to his car. His shoulders were squared and there was determination in his step. The warmth left by his touch lingered and her resolve threatened to weaken. Whether he's willing to admit it to himself or not, it's his love for his son that is motivating him, she again told herself and her resolve returned to its full strength.

Reseating herself at her desk, she glanced at her appointment calendar. But the paper blurred in front of her and she saw Jerome Sayer's angry face. Renewed concern for Lucas swept through her. She shrugged it off. Sayer was a bully. He would never physically take on anyone he thought could best him and Lucas Carver was a sturdy male specimen if ever she'd seen one.

She blinked her eyes back into focus. Her calendar was full. Not only was her morning booked but she had appointments through the afternoon. She would barely have time to make it home, change and be at Zebulon's by six. A smile spread over her face. There would be no time for Lucas Carver to occupy her mind.

Chapter Eight

Felicity had been wrong. Lucas had managed to slip into her thoughts during the day. Late in the afternoon, between appointments, she'd leaned back in her chair and closed her eyes for a moment. Immediately she'd found herself picturing him, Mark and Zebulon sitting on a huge boulder that extended out over the water. They were fishing. She could see Lucas's legs stretched out lazily in front of him, crossed at the ankles. The sunlight seemed to dance on the water while they all relaxed, shaded by a towering old elm tree and watched their corks floating gently. Scowling at this lapse of control, she'd jerked her mind back to her next appointment.

"My imagination has been working overtime," she mused, recalling the incident on the drive home. Never before had she visualized her thoughts so clearly. For a moment, she'd felt as if she was actually there with the men and boy by the lake.

Arriving home, the aroma of fresh blackberry cobbler greeted her. When she'd called to tell her grandmother she was going out for dinner, Thelma had informed her that Zebulon had come by that morning and invited her to join the rest of them for the fish fry.

The more the merrier, Felicity thought, giving her grandmother a hug of greeting then hurrying upstairs to change into her jeans. Having another person at the gathering made it even less likely she would be caught alone with Lucas. In the next instant, she was frowning at this bit of cowardliness. Even if they ended up alone she could resist him, she assured herself.

Her confidence was fully intact when she pulled up in front of Zebulon's house. Lucas was standing, waiting on the porch. Against her will, her gaze was drawn to him. He reminded her of an immovable mountain. The others, even her grandmother seated beside her, seem to fade until they were mere shadowy figures in a mist. Only she and Lucas remained clear and distinct, separate from the others as if in a world all their own.

Felicity closed her eyes tightly and when she opened them everyone else was again sharply in focus. I'm just tired. It's been a long day, she reasoned.

"Felicity!" Mark cried, rushing to the car to greet her.

She smiled warmly at the child. "Did you have fun today?" she asked.

He immediately launched into a garbled account of his fishing expedition. Because he was speaking faster now, but his words continued to be blurred, she had to concentrate hard to follow what he was saying. However, she managed to get a clear-enough idea to put in the "how nices" and "how excitings" when they were relevant.

"While Thelma helps me fry the fish, why don't you take Felicity for a walk down to the lake and show her where you caught them?" Zebulon suggested when Mark finally finished. "Your dad can go along just in case you run into a snake."

Felicity could barely believe her ears. Turning to Zebulon, she saw a twinkle in his eyes. He was playing the part of matchmaker! Never in a million years would she have pictured him in that role. She started to insist on helping with the preparation of the meal, when Mark slipped his hand into hers.

"Come," he said, looking very adult and self-important in his role as guide.

Not wanting to hurt the child's feelings, she obeyed. As Mark led the way and she followed, she was keenly aware of Lucas behind her. In spite of her attempts to ignore him, a slow burn that felt very much like the beginning of arousal spread through her.

She was fighting this disquieting reaction to his presence and losing when they reached the lake. Abruptly Lucas was forgotten as an acute sensation of déjà vu threatened to overwhelm her. She frowned in puzzlement. She'd never been to Zebulon's lake before. As Mark turned to the left and continued along the bank, she followed.

Behind her, Lucas had been thinking about how enticing Felicity looked in her jeans. And, the increasingly seductive sway of her hips had him convinced he was not imagining the growing heated excitement he was certain he detected radiating from her. Suddenly his more lecherous thoughts were being dampened by a flood of confusion. It was coming from Felicity.

Silently he laughed at himself. Here he was lusting after her and making himself believe she was feeling the same for him when, in reality, she was, no doubt totally oblivious to his company, trying to work out some legal problem that had arisen that day. Well, she wasn't going to evade him that easily. He would get her attention before this evening was over, he promised himself.

Ahead of them, Felicity saw the boulder and the shade tree. Shock swept through her. They were exactly as she'd pictured them this afternoon in her office.

Lucas nearly stumbled as the bolt of her shock jarred him. Forced to freeze in midstride to avoid running into her, he realized she was standing stiffly still.

Mark, who was quite a distance in front of them, was climbing up onto the boulder, gleefully gesturing with his hands and arms, describing how he'd caught his first fish.

"What's wrong?" Lucas demanded, scanning the ground and bushes for whatever had frightened Felicity into coming to such an abrupt halt.

"I'm not sure," she replied barely above a whisper.

Satisfied there was no immediate danger to either her or his son, Lucas relaxed enough to realize she wasn't frightened so much as wary and perplexed.

For the moment, Felicity could not move. All she could do was stand and stare.

Lucas stepped to the side so that he had a view of her face. She looked pale. "What has you so rattled?" he asked again.

"An unexpectedly strong feeling of déjà vu," she confessed. "I've never been here before and yet this afternoon—" Refusing to let him know she'd given even a moment's thought to him, she cut herself off in midsentence and gave her shoulders a shake in an effort to rid herself of the lingering shock seeing this place had caused. "A lot of lakes have rocks that jut out and are shaded by trees," she continued in a reasoning tone, talking as much to herself as to him. "And, I'm sure Zebulon has probably mentioned this spot to me before."

Lucas noted that the color had returned to her face. He also knew she wasn't telling him everything.

His scrutiny was like a physical touch and Felicity sensed the question in his mind. Well, he wasn't going to learn anymore from her. She waved to Mark. "We'd better be getting back. We don't want our dinner to get cold."

Nice evasive move, Lucas thought as the three started back to Zebulon's house. He was certain that whatever she hadn't said had involved him. The hint of a self-mocking smile played at one corner of his mouth. Or maybe he just wanted it to be about him. Maybe he just wanted to believe he'd managed to creep into her thoughts this afternoon.

Felicity managed to put the incident of déjà vu out of her mind for the remainder of the evening. The more difficult challenge was making certain she and Lucas were never alone. With both her grandmother and Zebulon attempting matchmaking, that hadn't been easy. But she had met the challenge and won.

She'd said her goodbyes and was on her way to the car when Thelma suddenly remembered she'd left her shawl in the house. "I'll go get it," Felicity offered, but Thelma had already started back into the house.

"Looks like we're finally alone," Lucas said.

Felicity turned to discover him standing only a couple of feet away. Mark and Zebulon had followed Thelma into the house to help her look for her wrap.

"You've been avoiding me all evening," he continued, taking another step closer. "I'm betting that you're worried I might be able to melt those icy barriers you want to keep between us, if you let me get too close."

He wants a mother for his son, she repeated silently over and over again, trying not to notice how tempting he looked. Still, her hands itched to test the feel of his shoulders. She shoved them into the pockets of her jeans to make certain they did not act of their own accord.

"You're too young and vital to live out your life alone," he said gruffly, gently combing a strand of hair back behind her ear with the tip of his finger.

His touch sent currents of excitement coursing through her. She'd never felt so strong an attraction toward any man before and the intensity of her feelings frightened her. She forced herself to remember the dark, depressing days when she'd realized Jeff no longer loved her. She couldn't bear the thought of going through those terrible, hurtful emotions of betrayal and failure again and, most certainly, not with a man who could arouse such intense reactions within her. "I might consider falling in love again but it won't be with a man who chooses me because his son has chosen me for a mother."

Lucas frowned down at her. "I'm comfortable and secure in my role as a single parent, and I do not lie to myself. I chose you because I've never been this attracted to a woman in my life."

Her body wanted to melt into his arms. "Attractions fade," she said, more to herself than to him.

"Not this one," he assured her huskily. "It's growing with each passing moment." He cupped her face in his hands. "I'm not a frivolous man. Fact is, I'm normally very conservative. And I'll admit, I'm shocked by how strongly I've felt about you from the first time I saw you. You have this incredible hold over me."

His breath was teasing her skin. She knew he was going to kiss her. She ordered herself to pull away but her legs refused to respond. Then his mouth found hers. Her first awareness was of gentleness and warmth. Then came strength as his hands left her face and traveled over her shoulders to close around her upper arms. Her body was not even touching his and yet she was as aware of him as if he were holding her pressed tightly against him.

"We belong together," he said seductively against her lips.

A responding yes formed in her mind.

"Felicity be my mother?" an excited young voice interrupted.

Lucas had known she was close to surrender. Now he felt her guard once again in place. She took a backward step, and he was forced to release her.

Shaken by how close she'd come to succumbing to the lust he awoke in her, for a moment Felicity could not speak. But as she looked down at Mark's face and saw the hopefulness there, her mind cleared. Whether Lucas knew it or not, he was doing this for his son. Even she found it extremely difficult to deny the boy's plea. I'd probably convince myself I was in love with someone if I had a child who wanted the match as much as

Mark wants this one, she admitted. Kneeling in front of the boy, she gave him a hug. "Let's be friends," she said firmly.

His disappointment was evident.

Lucas laid a hand on his son's shoulder. "Friendship is a precious and important commodity."

The boy looked up at his father questioningly. "Coommmoodie?"

"Something we want," Lucas replied simply.

"Will you be my friend?" Felicity asked the boy coaxingly.

He grimaced with regret, then nodded and hugged her.

"Go say goodbye to Mrs. Burrow," Lucas instructed.

When the boy left to obey and Felicity straightened, Lucas reached out and touched her lightly on the cheek. "I don't give up easily," he warned quietly for her ears only.

She had to again force herself to remember the sense of personal failure she'd experienced when her marriage to Jeff fell apart. Quickly she hurried to thank Zebulon for the meal, then ushered her grandmother into the car.

"We certainly got out of there fast," Thelma remarked as they drove home. "Someone might get the impression you were running scared."

Felicity drew a terse breath. "Maybe I am."

"The question is, who are you running from... yourself or Lucas?" her grandmother asked.

"Maybe both."

Thelma frowned. "Running away from yourself never works. And running away from Lucas may prove to be one of the most foolish things you've ever done. He's a good man."

"I know. I know." Felicity's jaw firmed. "But I'm not taking a chance on making another mistake. I can't face that kind of failure again."

"You didn't fail," her grandmother said sternly.

Felicity's jaw hardened even more. "Maybe not, but it sure felt like I did." As she parked in front of their house, the thought that her grandmother could be right and she could be passing up an opportunity for happiness tormented her. "How can I know for sure it's me Lucas really wants and not just a mother for his son?"

"You're going to have to trust your instincts," her grandmother replied.

Felicity gave her a dry look. "I did that the first time." Resolve etched itself into her features. "I'm not taking that risk again. Better safe than sorry."

"In this case, you may be sorry you played it safe," Thelma warned, climbing out of the car.

Felicity let out a mental shriek of frustration as she followed her grandmother inside.

Lucas was pulling out of Zebulon's driveway when a sharp jolt of frustration pierced him. Surprised, he glanced at his son to find that Mark had already fallen asleep. Where, he wondered, had that burst of emotion come from? Felicity immediately entered his mind. He frowned. He'd never received such strong, definitive emotional impressions from a distance before. However, he did seem to be unusually attuned to her.

Again a self-mocking smile tilted one corner of his mouth. Or maybe he simply wanted to believe the frustration had come from her. Forcing himself to face re-

ality, he had to admit that it had, most likely, come
from within him. Tonight when he'd kissed her, he'd
hoped he could destroy the barrier she kept between
them. But he hadn't succeeded. He had come very close,
though, he reminded himself.

Later when he climbed into bed and closed his eyes,
he recalled how sweet she'd tasted. The remembered
heat of her lips caused a warmth to spread through him
and he fell asleep thinking about her.

Felicity moaned with pleasure and ran her hand over
the muscular chest of the man who held her. She looked
up and was not surprised to discover her lover was Lucas Carver. He kissed her shoulder, then trailed kisses
to her neck and finally found her mouth.

Her breathing became more rapid. The sheet was a
hindrance and she kicked it off as she moved more fully
into his arms.

Then suddenly her lover was gone. Startled by the
unexpected desertion, she sat up. The movement jarred
her awake.

"I cannot believe I had another dream about that
man," she growled at herself.

Her breathing was still ragged and a sense of being
unfulfilled nagged her. Grudgingly she confessed that
what had her truly unnerved was how real the dream
had felt.

"I also can't believe how sexually frustrated I feel
simply because I woke before it ended," she grumbled.

Her mind flashed back and she frowned. That wasn't
exactly true. Even if she were still asleep, she'd be feeling frustrated and unfulfilled. The reason she'd woken
was that Lucas had suddenly vanished from her arms.

As she became more awake an unsettling thought nagged her. Just before he'd disappeared, she'd thought she heard a child's cry.

"Lucas's kiss and Mark's soulful gaze have my imagination working overtime," she admonished herself.

A headache was building and she climbed out of bed and took a couple of aspirins. Then ordering herself not to think of Lucas, she lay down and went back to sleep.

Chapter Nine

Lucas sat drinking his second cup of coffee while Mark finished his cereal. He felt restless, and he knew why. Sometime in the middle of the night, his son had woken him for a glass of water. He normally didn't mind that kind of interruption but he'd been dreaming about Felicity. When he'd gone back to sleep he'd tried to recapture the dream, but it was gone. Better to have the real thing anyway, he told himself.

Looking out the window, he frowned thoughtfully. From the moment he'd driven into Smytheshire, he'd liked the feel of the town. Now he found himself thinking that he would enjoy making this his permanent home.

"We're going to do a little business today, son," he announced. "Your grandfather likes running his own bank. He gives me some responsibility but we've knocked heads more often than not." Reaching across the table, he ruffled the boy's hair. "It's time I struck out on my own."

"We see Felicity?" Mark asked hopefully.

"Most definitely," Lucas promised.

Felicity had not been surprised when she received an early-morning call from Zebulon asking her to come by his place at her earliest convenience. She hadn't had an appointment scheduled until ten so she'd stopped by before going into town. He'd informed her that he wanted a new will, leaving everything to Lucas. After seeing the old man with his great-grandson and great-great-grandson, Felicity had expected this. Now as she drew up the papers, the realization that she could find herself with Lucas Carver as a neighbor dawned on her.

He'd never choose to live here, she assured herself. Seattle was his home.

Recalling the dream she'd had last night, a nervousness swept through her. The man, she admitted, was a threat to her resolve. The sooner he left town, the better.

A knock on her office door startled her. Peggy, she knew, was using her lunch hour to run errands in town. Obviously a client had come in who didn't want to wait. She started to rise, but before she was halfway out of her chair, the door was opened and Lucas entered with Mark.

"We were on our way to have lunch at the café when we ran into your secretary," Lucas said. "She told us you were working through your lunch break, and she would bring you a sandwich when she returned to the office. Since it's already nearly one and we didn't want you to have to gulp down your food, we volunteered to bring it for her and join you." He began taking out their lunches as he talked.

Felicity's heart skipped a beat. He looked close to irresistible. She swung her attention to Mark. "I'm really very busy," she said, with apology. She didn't want the boy to feel unwanted, but she also didn't want to spend time with Lucas.

"You have to eat and all the new studies claim that it's healthier to eat with others than to eat alone," Lucas insisted, seating his son at the small round table by the window and placing one of the sandwiches in front of him.

"You eat?" Mark coaxed.

Realizing Lucas was not going to give her a choice, Felicity capitulated. "I'll eat."

Mark grinned with relief and took a bite of his sandwich.

A concern that had been nagging at the back of Lucas's mind began to taunt him again. He'd told himself it was an obstacle he could overcome. Still, he wanted to know what he was up against. As he placed Felicity's sandwich down in front of her, he leaned across the desk until their faces were only inches apart. Then in a voice low enough for his son not to be able to discern the words, he asked tersely, "Are you still in love with Lomax?"

She scowled. "No."

He sensed no hesitation and smiled. "Even if you'd thought you were, I know I'm the man for you. I'd just have to work a little harder to convince you of that."

The determination she saw in his eyes made her toes want to curl. No curling toes! she admonished herself. I won't be fooled again. What he really means is that I'm the mother he wants for his child.

"Felicity?" Mark spoke her name with concern.

She glanced to the child to find him watching her. She and Lucas had kept their voices low and although she'd scowled briefly, she'd quickly returned her expression to one of neutrality; yet Mark had clearly sensed her conflict. Apparently he had inherited some of his father's ability to detect emotions in others. "Your father and I were just having a small disagreement," she said. "It's nothing for you to worry about."

Lucas continued to regard her narrowly. He'd had a flash of curling toes... very cute toes encased in nylons. Then had come a sharp image of his son and Felicity. She was in an apron in a kitchen and Mark was standing beside her. A suspicion that had been building in the back of his mind insisted on being investigated.

If he was right, this new development was somewhat unnerving. It also added proof to Zebulon's story of his heritage and, obviously, Felicity's as well. Or, I could be getting as loony as the old man, he mocked himself. Still, he could not overlook the possibility of what was happening. He had to know the truth.

Feeling a prickling on his neck, he glanced over his shoulder to find his son regarding him questioningly. "Felicity's right. There is nothing for you to worry about," he assured the boy.

Mark nodded and returned to eating.

As Lucas seated himself in one of the chairs in front of her desk and opened the container holding his sandwich, Felicity could feel him covertly studying her. There was a curiosity in his eyes as if he'd suddenly discovered something that puzzled him.

"I wish you'd quit looking at me as if I had a third eye in my forehead," she said in hushed tones Mark could not hear.

"Maybe in a way you do," he replied cryptically. "Maybe we both do."

She wanted to know what he meant by that remark but Mark suddenly popped into her mind and the thought that this was not the time to ask kept her silent. Trying to ignore Lucas, she turned her full attention to the child. "I suppose you'll be glad to get back home soon," she said, hoping to discover they were planning to leave in the next day or so.

Mark smiled brightly. "We stay."

There was a finality in his words that made her uneasy. Her attention swung back to Lucas. "Surely you have to be getting back to work."

"I do have to be getting back to work," he agreed.

Felicity sensed there was something he wasn't telling her. She started to probe but Mark again came into her mind, followed by the thought that it would be prudent to wait. Again, she remained silent. But as Lucas returned to eating his sandwich, she studied him narrowly. He was sitting in a relaxed posture with his legs stretched out in front of him, crossed at the ankles. He looked like a man with nothing in particular on his mind. Well, he couldn't fool her. She knew without a doubt his manner was designed to put her off her guard. There was something going on.

As she took another bite of her sandwich, her gaze left his face to travel along the line of his body. Immediately she realized that was a mistake. A fire began to flame within her.

Abruptly he straightened and rose. Setting his partially eaten sandwich aside, he strode to the window and looked out.

Felicity suddenly thought of a cold shower. That's exactly what I need, she told herself, furious that he could so easily arouse her. There would be no more "swept off her feet" type of romance in her life.

"Your secretary is returning," Lucas announced breaking into her thoughts. He strode to where his son was sitting. "I need to talk to Felicity alone. I want you to finish eating your lunch with Mrs. Cassidy."

Mark looked as if he was going to protest.

"This is important," Lucas said firmly.

Mark shrugged, then nodded his consent.

Felicity was about to say that she saw no reason for Mark to leave, when Lucas glanced her way with a warning on his face. Clearly he had something to say to her that could not be said in front of the boy. And, knowing his persistence, she decided she might as well hear it now. If she didn't, he was sure to seek her out later. "See you in a little while," she called out to Mark as his father ushered him out of the room. Then pressing the intercom button on her phone, she asked Peggy to watch the boy. "And let me know the minute my two o'clock appointment arrives," she finished.

"Mrs. Elberly canceled," Peggy replied. "I meant to tell you but another call came in almost immediately. Then Mr. Carver called and wanted an appointment so I gave him the two o'clock spot. I just never got a chance to pencil it in on your schedule."

Felicity managed a stiff thank you as Lucas returned to her office and closed the door.

"I need a lawyer," he said, easing himself into the chair across from her desk. Again he stretched his legs out in front of him and crossed them at the ankle as if totally relaxed. But there was nothing relaxed in the way his gaze focused on her.

She felt as if he were trying to see into her very soul. "And why do you need a lawyer?" she asked, the question coming out curtly instead of with her usual professional calm.

"First I have a question for you." His gaze narrowed even more. "A little while ago, did you think of your toes curling?"

Felicity flushed. "No, of course not."

Triumph flashed in his eyes. "You're lying." He frowned thoughtfully. "What I don't understand is you in a kitchen with Mark."

Felicity stared at him in stunned disbelief.

"Wait, don't tell me." He rose to his feet in one lithe movement, placed his hands on her desk and leaned toward her. "The curling toes were because you were experiencing a strong attraction to me. You fought the attraction again by telling yourself that I wanted you as a mother for Mark, thus the domestic scene."

"How could you know exactly what I was thinking?" Felicity demanded shakily.

He frowned thoughtfully. "I got a flash of curling toes and then that image of you and Mark." A mischievous grin tilted one corner of his mouth. "Just before Peggy arrived, while you were supposedly ignoring me, I had a very lecherous glimpse of you and me."

Felicity was too shaken to be embarrassed. "You read my mind?"

"I wouldn't call it reading. It's more like quick images."

Felicity recalled something. "The cold shower. That wasn't my idea. And twice I was going to ask you something but was stopped by the thought that it would not be wise to speak in front of Mark.''

''The cold shower was my thought as well as the warnings,'' Lucas admitted. ''Apparently this ability works both ways. I suspected it might.''

Felicity suddenly recalled seeing the men fishing the day before. She hadn't *seen* Lucas. She'd seen his feet and legs...she'd seen what he'd been seeing. ''This isn't possible,'' she snapped.

''Why were you thinking about us fishing?'' Lucas demanded. Then a look as if a light bulb had just come on in his brain came over his features. ''That incident of déjà vu at the lake that had you so shaken yesterday...it wasn't déjà vu. You'd had an image flash just like the ones I had today.''

Felicity was still trying to sort out what was going on. ''I was actually seeing what you were seeing. This has never happened to me before.''

''Me neither,'' Lucas admitted. A sudden realization occurred to him. ''Weren't you in your office yesterday afternoon?''

''Yes.'' As it occurred to her where this question was leading, her uneasiness increased.

''You received my thoughts all the way from Zebulon's place to here,'' he said with amazement.

Felicity glared at him. ''I don't want you in my mind! My thoughts are private!''

''I don't think it's a matter of being *in* your mind. If I was in there then I'd know what you were actually thinking and I don't, not really. All I get is pictures and emotions.''

Other than a feeling of peacefulness, Felicity realized that she'd had no idea what he was thinking when she'd received the image from the lake, and she calmed slightly. "I still don't like this," she said stiffly.

"It will certainly make surprising you on special occasions difficult," he mused.

Felicity continued to have trouble accepting what was happening. Frantically, she searched for an explanation. "You did say you've always had a knack for telling if someone was lying." Recalling how positive he'd been when he'd said he knew she was attracted to him, she added, "And I assume that includes sensing other emotions as well . . . likes, dislikes, et cetera?"

He nodded.

"We seem to have the same ability. That could mean our brains are operating on the same wavelength," she concluded.

"So it would seem."

Mark's face suddenly entered Felicity's mind.

"I'm fairly certain my son has inherited this same ability to discern emotions in others that we both share," Lucas said, already heading for the door. "I wonder if he is as attuned to us as we are to each other."

Felicity merely smiled a greeting when he brought the boy into the room. None of this seemed really possible. Maybe it was one of those very realistic nightmares, she thought hopefully. But she knew it wasn't.

"We're going to play a game," Lucas told Mark, seating his son in the chair in front of Felicity's desk. "I'm going to think of a toy, and I want you to tell me what it is."

Mark grinned, clearly happy to be with his father and Felicity and especially to be playing a game.

Felicity saw the ragged teddy bear as clearly as if it were sitting on the desk in front of her. But Mark simply kept grinning at his father as if waiting for the game to begin.

"Do you know what toy I'm thinking about?" Lucas prodded.

"A train," Mark replied hopefully.

"No, but you did great." Lucas smiled reassuringly at the boy, then turned to Felicity. "Why don't you think of a toy and see if he can guess."

She thought of a green ball she used to play with when she was his age.

"A doll?" Mark guessed.

Felicity shook her head.

Mark looked distressed.

"It's all right," she said quickly, rising and coming around the desk to ruffle his hair playfully. This was not a lie...she was having a hard enough time dealing with the fact that the boy's father was receiving messages from her that she didn't want to send. She didn't need a third party receiving them as well.

The boy smiled with relief, clearly realizing she wasn't lying.

"Felicity and I have some more business we need to discuss," Lucas said, picking up his son and carrying him to the door.

Felicity felt Mark's disappointment and gave him an encouraging wink. She sensed his spirits lift and inside experienced a warm glow that she'd been able to make the boy happy with a simple look. Don't get too attached to him, she cautioned herself. If she did, she might be able to convince herself that marrying Lucas for his son's sake was not such a bad idea. And that could prove disastrous.

Returning to her office alone, Lucas closed the door, then crossed the room and seated himself in the chair his son had recently occupied. "It seems these image exchanges are a special bond between you and me," he said in an easy drawl.

Felicity dropped her head onto her desk. "This can't be happening."

"I'm finding it a bit of a shock myself, but it's not the worst thing that could happen," Lucas growled.

Still resting her forehead on her desk, she met his anger with a groan of frustration. "I don't want there to be a special bond between us. I want you out of my life. I let my hormones talk me into one mistake, I refuse to let them win again."

Lucas could feel her inner struggle. The thought of taking her in his arms and kissing her as a way to turn the battle in his favor played through his mind.

Her head jerked up. "No!" she growled, bracing herself for a fight.

Lucas immediately discarded that image from his mind. But it had sparked other memories. "Speaking of hormones," he said, watching her closely, "have you been having any erotic dreams lately?"

Her and Lucas as lovers came back vividly into Felicity's mind.

He grinned. "Yes, those are the ones."

"I'll thank you not to send me any more of those," she snapped.

He cocked an eyebrow. "What makes you think I was the one who sent them? Maybe you're the originator. My imagination has never been that good in the past."

Felicity glared at him. "Nor mine!"

"Then it would seem that together we make quite a team," he concluded.

Her jaw tensed. "It's just lust," she said curtly. "And marriages built on that don't last."

"You are a hardheaded woman," he mused. "What can I do to prove we would make a terrific pair?"

Felicity rested her elbows on her desk and cupped her face in her hands. "You would have to be my friend first. I'd have to have time to learn to trust you. That could take months, maybe years."

He straightened. "Taking my time isn't going to be easy," he said. "However, I'm prepared to do just that."

She stared at him in surprise. She'd been being totally honest about the length of time courting her could take and she'd expected him to, at least, waver in his resolve. "Don't you have to be getting home soon?"

"We have now come to the reason I need a lawyer. I spoke to Theodore Smythe this morning. He has agreed to allow me to buy into his family's bank." A thoughtful expression came over his features as he recalled what Zebulon had told him about the founding of the town. "It seems that my being related to Zebulon counts a great deal with the Smythes."

"You're buying into the bank? You're planning to stay here in Smytheshire?" she gasped.

"Mark and I like it here."

Felicity noted that he had mentioned his son. He would do anything for the boy, she reminded herself, determined not to be deceived.

Lucas scowled as he sensed her barrier strengthening. Hoping to weaken it, he pictured himself gently touching her face. Then, in his mind, he leaned closer to kiss her lightly on the nose. But before he reached her, she disappeared behind a solid wooden wall.

Felicity grinned triumphantly. "Apparently there are ways of maintaining my privacy."

"You're incredibly cute when you win a round. Your eyes sparkle and you wrinkle your nose just a smidgen," he observed good-naturedly. "I'm going to enjoy having you as my lawyer."

"I really don't think—" she began to protest.

"I'm accepting your rules... first, we get to know each other and become friends." He interrupted. "It's only fair that you play."

Playing with him sounded like much too much fun.

"Besides, you have to be my lawyer," he persisted. "You're the best according to Zebulon. And I only work with the best."

"Flattery will get you nowhere with me, Lucas Carver," she warned.

He grinned. "But ethics will. I want you for my lawyer and you can't, in good conscience, send me to anyone else."

She frowned at his determination. "I'm not an expert on corporate law."

His manner became businesslike. "I want a local lawyer, someone I can work closely with and someone who can handle all of my legal needs. However, I'll have a corporate attorney you recommend take a look at the contract. The deal I've struck is straightforward, and I'm familiar with the government regulations. I don't think there should be any problems. But, if there are, I want you there to help me with the negotiations."

She knew that no one else in town would be more thorough than herself. Even more, there was a part of her that wanted to be certain his interests were protected. She'd feel the same about anyone who came to her for help, she assured herself. "Are you really certain you want to go through with this deal?" she asked, the lawyer side of her taking over. "It's a big step. Maybe you should take a little longer to consider."

"I'll admit I only took a cursory glance through their books, but the figures indicate that the Bank of Smytheshire is one of the most solid institutions I've ever encountered. Besides, my intuition tells me this is an excellent business deal. I've always fared well when I've trusted my instincts."

Felicity knew the bank was rock solid. Both she and her grandfather had had business dealings with the institution. Still, she was not prepared to accept this turn of events so easily. "Even so, I would never advise any client of mine to relocate on a whim," she argued.

His gaze leveled on her. "This is no whim. I know what I want."

"People don't always get what they want," she cautioned.

"And some people pass up opportunities they regret later," he returned. Rising to his feet, he leaned across the desk and caught her chin in his hand. "A friend wouldn't let that happen to a friend."

Felicity found herself being drawn into the blue depths of his eyes. The two of them having a picnic in a meadow filled with wildflowers filled her mind. The summer sun was warming them and there was a lazy feeling in the air. Slowly he began drawing her into his arms. Suddenly realizing what was happening, she scowled. Two can play this game, she mused.

An expression of shock came over Lucas's face as a swarm of bees descended into the meadow and sent the picnickers scurrying.

Releasing her chin, he straightened and grinned. "Bees. Really, Felicity. A rain shower would have sufficed."

"I don't think so," she replied, the image of the two of them, their clothing soaked and clinging seductively to their bodies filling her mind.

"Well, maybe not," he agreed huskily. His grin returned. "I'm going to enjoy matching wits with you."

Felicity recalled the restlessness she'd felt the day he'd first come to town. Clearly he'd been the source. "I should have known from the first time our paths crossed that you would be trouble."

"What I am is your future," he stated. Before she could protest, his manner became businesslike. "I've asked the Smythes to have their lawyer deliver the agreement to your office. In the meantime, I need to fly back to Seattle and make arrangements to borrow the money I'll need to close the deal."

Felicity breathed a mental sigh of relief as she accompanied him into the reception area to say goodbye to Mark. A few days without Lucas in town would give her time to rebuild her defenses.

But standing on the porch waving goodbye, the aching sadness of parting with someone she hated to see go descended over her. It was Mark she would miss, she assured herself. His bright smile always gave her pleasure.

However, later that evening sitting on the porch swing of her grandmother's house and gazing up at the star-filled sky, it wasn't Mark who was on her mind. She'd been fighting thinking of Lucas ever since he'd left. Giving up the struggle, she guessed he and Mark were probably in a plane winging their way home by now. Hoping their flight was smooth, she leaned back and closed her eyes.

Abruptly she was seeing the interior of an airliner. In front of her was an open magazine and Mark was asleep in the seat to her left. Suddenly her view was a panorama of the aisle and the nearby seats as if she was looking for something. Then it settled on the seat in front of her and everything went blank. She knew Lucas had leaned back and closed his eyes.

Miss me?

Felicity's eyes popped open. Those words had come from Lucas. Even though he was hundreds of miles away, her mind had linked with his! And he'd known she was there. But what truly stunned her was that he'd sent a message . . . not an image but a verbal message.

Feeling as if someone had joined her on the porch, she opened her eyes expecting to see her grandmother. Instead she was still alone.

Felicity?

It was Lucas, again. So that was the reason behind his sudden glance around the cabin of the plane. He'd sensed someone approaching him just as she'd thought she'd sensed another presence on the porch. *I was just hoping you and Mark were having a good flight,* she replied, then used her image of a door closing between them to block off any further communications.

In her mind she heard a rapping sound and pictured him knocking against the barrier. *Good night, Mr. Carver,* she thought with stern determination.

The rapping stopped. *Sleep tight, Felicity,* came the reply. Then once again she was alone.

Felicity raked her hands through her hair. What was happening between her and Lucas Carver was impossible. Even if someone she knew and trusted had told her they were experiencing this kind of phenomenon, she would have thought they were hallucinating or that their elevator suddenly wasn't going all the way to the top floor.

Mentally she reconstructed the barrier between her and Lucas. When she finished it looked like the door of a dungeon in an ancient castle. It was solid oak, six inches thick with huge iron hinges. Inserting a large iron key, she locked it.

Lucas leaned back in his seat and closed his eyes. Again he sought out Felicity only to find himself looking at an impenetrable door.

Deciding that she probably needed some time alone to adjust to this new development, he returned his mind to the plane. That he should be somewhat stunned himself occurred to him. And he was. When he'd first sensed a strong presence nearby in the plane, he'd been sure the stewardess was approaching or one of the passengers had become agitated. After he'd assured himself that wasn't the case, he'd realized there was a very familiar aura about the presence. Then he'd become aware of a warm summer breeze and smelled fragrant mountain air. He still hadn't been sure Felicity was the one he was sensing. Asking if she was missing him had been a wishful thought. He hadn't expected her to hear it.

When her shock had been transmitted back to him, he'd been equally startled. And when he'd heard her answer, he'd been too stunned to respond before she managed to close the door between them, forcing him to communicate through the barrier.

Contemplating this new quirk to their link, he discovered that he actually felt more comfortable about the whole situation. After he'd left Felicity's office, the thought that she could see through his eyes whenever she pleased and he might not know she was there, had nagged at him. He'd even considered constructing a door similar to the one she'd first used. But he hadn't. He'd simply ordered his mind to be more aware of any visitors. And, although he hadn't immediately known who had approached him, he'd been instantly conscious of her presence.

Thinking back to the afternoon he and Mark had been fishing with Zebulon, he realized he'd sensed her presence then as well. The scent of her soft perfume had suddenly filled his senses as he'd watched his son fishing. He'd even glanced around to see if she'd come up the path unexpectedly.

A lopsided grin spread over his face. If he wasn't so certain of his own sanity, he'd begin to think he was missing a few rungs from his ladder. This mental connection he had with Felicity Burrow didn't seem possible. Yet, it was happening. What was even more amazing was that it felt natural, as if a part of himself that had been lying dormant was now suddenly awake and functioning.

He'd gone to Smytheshire hoping to find some clue that would cure his son's reticence. He hadn't expected to discover he had ancestors who possessed extraordinary, extrasensory powers. And he most certainly had not expected to find the key that would not only unlock his son's determined muteness but would also unlock a part of himself he'd never known existed. But he had and Felicity was that key. Now he simply had to convince her that a key without the lock it fits is useless and vice versa.

Chapter Ten

Parking in front of Mrs. Elberly's home the next morning, Felicity glanced at her watch. It was nine o'clock. She was right on time. It was not unusual for her to make housecalls to accommodate her more elderly clients. However, she did not meet with clients on a Saturday unless it was an emergency. This was her day to sit alone in her office and catch up on any work not done during the week. But today she hadn't wanted to be alone. It was too easy to let herself begin to think about Lucas.

"It's so sweet of you to come," the elderly lady greeted her at the door.

"I'll just put the tea and pastries on the coffee table, then be on my way," a younger female voice said from behind Mrs. Elberly.

Felicity looked down the hall to see Gillian Hudson, Mrs. Elberly's grandniece, carrying a heavily loaded tray. Gillian, like Felicity, was in her late twenties. Long brown hair hung several inches below her shoulders, her eyes were a dark, hickory brown, and her features were well formed. She would be very pretty if she'd fix herself up some, Felicity thought for the umpteenth time.

Gillian had been born and raised in California and, until she'd moved in with her grandaunt, only came to Smytheshire on occasional visits. In years past, the hickory-eyed woman had taken pains with her appearance and captured the attention of several of the more eligible men when she was in town.

But these days, Gillian wore no makeup. As for her hair, it was either hanging straight in a nondescript style or pulled back into a ponytail. And the clothes she chose could only be classified as dowdy. Felicity had also noticed that Gillian tended to avoid social gatherings. When they couldn't be avoided, she stayed in the background.

Felicity had sensed a tremendous sadness mingled with anxiousness within Gillian when the woman had first moved in with Wanda Elberly. Now, Gillian seemed much more relaxed. Still, she behaved with a shyness that kept her in the shadows. She made her living writing romance novels and, Felicity thought with regret for the young woman, she had become the epitome of the reclusive author.

"Gillian, dear, why don't you join us for a cup of tea before you go running off?" Mrs. Elberly coaxed.

Gillian smiled warmly at the elderly woman. "Thank you, but you and Felicity have business to discuss and I really need to get my errands done." She paused long enough to help the arthritic old woman into a chair, then quickly left the room.

A moment later Felicity heard the front door closing.

"I'm so glad that girl came to stay with me," Mrs. Elberly remarked.

The vibrations she sensed from both women left no doubt in Felicity's mind there was true affection between the elderly aunt and her distant niece. And those in town who knew Mrs. Elberly had breathed a sigh of relief when Gillian had come here to live a couple of years ago. A while before that, a storm had blown a tree over on Mrs. Elberly's house. The old woman had not been injured but she had been badly shaken and friends had been concerned about her remaining alone.

Mrs. Elberly waved toward the sofa. "Have some tea and I'll tell you how I want my will reworded."

A few minutes later, Felicity was jotting down Mrs. Elberly's instructions when she heard a knock. Pausing she glanced over her shoulder in the direction of the hall.

"Is something wrong, dear?" Mrs. Elberly asked.

"I thought I heard a knock on the door," Felicity replied, realizing even as she spoke that Mrs. Elberly's front door wasn't where the knocking had come from.

Mrs. Elberly frowned in puzzlement. "I didn't hear any knocking." She suddenly smiled. "My crystals are certainly singing a merry tune, though."

Felicity glanced toward the collection of geodes and crystalline structures on the table by the window. Placed to catch the sun's rays, some merely sparkled while others cast rainbows on a nearby wall. They did look cheerful, she thought. Then the knocking sounded again. She closed her eyes. A dungeon door filled her inner vision. The banging continued. *Go away. I'm with a client!* she thought curtly.

The knocking stopped.

"Are you all right, dear?"

Felicity opened her eyes to discover Mrs. Elberly watching her worriedly. "I'm fine. It was just one of those little nuisance headaches a person gets once in a while."

"The crystals aren't singing anymore," Mrs. Elberly noted with disappointment.

Felicity had always known that the woman honestly believed she heard music of various sorts from her crystals. But like the other residents in town, she'd been sure that whatever Mrs. Elberly heard was due to faulty hearing aids or a very vivid imagination. However, now that Lucas had come knocking on her mental door, she wasn't so sure the old woman's crystals didn't sing to her. "You were saying you want to leave this house and its contents, including your crystals, to Gillian," she said, determined to return to more practical thoughts.

The old woman nodded. "Yes. As you know, my son and his wife are long since dead and buried. They had no offspring and no one else in the family is interested in living here in Smytheshire. But this must be our little secret. Gillian would be embarrassed if she was to learn of my bequest. She didn't come here seeking anything from me except for sanctuary."

Mrs. Elberly suddenly clamped her mouth shut, clearly worried she'd said too much.

"Anything you tell me during a consultation is strictly confidential," Felicity assured her.

"It'd be best if you'd just forget that last little bit," Mrs. Elberly coaxed with a plea.

Felicity smiled her most reassuring smile. "Consider it forgotten."

The elderly woman visibly relaxed, then continued with her instructions.

A couple of hours later, Felicity was sitting in her office nibbling on a pastry Mrs. Elberly had insisted she take and wondering why Gillian Hudson needed a sanctuary. It's probably got something to do with a man, she mused dryly, as the knocking on her dungeon door sounded again. They can be persistent pests, she grumbled. Still, she could not resist the urge to open the door. Immediately Lucas's presence filled her mind.

I thought you might like to meet my family, he offered.

Her cautious side ordered her to close the door. But she was curious. Besides, seeing them through his eyes wasn't the same as being taken home to meet his parents, she reasoned. Unless... *You haven't told them about our being able to communicate?* she demanded, shaken by this thought. Afraid that even her grandmother might have trouble accepting this newfound ability, she hadn't even told Thelma.

No, he replied with a small laugh. *They'd be certain I'd come unhinged.*

Felicity relaxed somewhat. In the next instant, she was looking at two women. The younger one, whom she judged to be in her early fifties, was slender and dressed in white slacks and a lightweight white sweater with red and yellow flowers embroidered upon it. Her face was pretty and her eyes were the same color of blue as Lucas's. She'd been standing at a sideboard where food was laid out. It looked like a breakfast assortment and Felicity realized Lucas was three hours behind her. As she watched, the woman left the sideboard and sat down at the end of a long dining table. *My mother, Joline Carver,* Lucas informed her.

The second woman, an older version of Joline Carver, had remained sitting at the table while a maid served her. A long, double strand of pearls hung around her neck and the lightweight floral print dress she wore was clearly of the finest quality. *My maternal grandmother, Camille Maxwell,* Lucas clarified.

This was Zebulon's daughter, Felicity realized and studied the older woman more closely.

The maid suddenly moved into view, and Felicity again became aware of the room in which the women and Lucas were eating. It had an air of aristocratic elegance that only came from old money. For the first time, she realized just how well-to-do his family truly was. She thought of her grandmother's warm, cozy kitchen and suddenly felt out of place looking in on his life.

Surely you're not going to let a little wealth intimidate you, he chided. *Besides, this is my parents' house. I'm in the process of putting my money into a business. There will be no live-in maids for us for a while. Well, maybe one. I want you to have time for me.*

And especially time for your son, she added, determined never to forget Mark's role in this courtship.

Especially time for me. He corrected her.

Abruptly her mind was again filled with the image of herself and Lucas curled up on the couch in the large living room with the brick fireplace. *That's your home, I've been seeing,* she blurted, stunned by this revelation.

Obviously our minds began melding long before we realized, he mused. His thoughts reached out to touch her like a mental caress. *Without you, the home you are seeing now feels like a cold, empty abode. I'm moving to Smytheshire because I need you by my side to make me feel complete.*

The urge to believe him was strong. But she'd been fooled once and she would not play that role twice.

"I really don't understand why you feel you have to buy into another bank. We have several," a woman's voice suddenly entered Felicity's mind.

"Because those banks are run as a whole by the family, with Dad and his brothers holding the reins. I want to be on my own," she heard Lucas reply.

"Your father will be retiring soon. You'll need to take over his seat on the board," the female voice argued.

Lucas had turned to the woman who was speaking. It was his mother, Joline Carver.

"Ahem!" A masculine voice interrupted. "I have no intentions of retiring any day soon."

An older version of Lucas was now in Felicity's line of vision. "And you shouldn't," Lucas was saying. "No one can run the business better than you."

The older man smiled with satisfaction and nodded. "I appreciate the vote of confidence, son." His expression became serious. "And perhaps it is best if you went out on your own. I know we haven't seen eye to eye on several things lately. I think you need to try your wings. And this Bank of Smytheshire looks like a good solid investment. I've checked into it."

"But why Smytheshire?" Joline demanded. "If you must have your independence, why not buy into a bank that's closer? Surely you're not doing this simply to be near that woman you've become enamored with."

"I like Smytheshire," Lucas replied firmly.

"I'd like to go there and meet Zebulon," an elderly voice Felicity had not yet heard, spoke up. Now she found herself looking at his grandmother, Camille Maxwell.

"As soon as Mark and I are settled, you're welcome to come visit anytime," Lucas invited. Felicity suddenly sensed hesitation on his part, then heard him add, "However, as I've warned you, he's a little eccentric. But I like him."

"You've always shown good judgment where people are concerned," Camille noted, then returned to eating.

"About this woman, Felicity Burrow," Lucas's mother interjected, her tone indicating worry. "You barely know her. How can you be so sure she's the right wife for you? What if you buy this bank and then discover you've made a mistake?"

"I haven't made a mistake," Lucas replied firmly.

"I knew your grandfather was the man for me, the first moment I saw him," Camille spoke up again.

"Lucas has a practical head on his shoulders." This was his father speaking again, addressing Joline. "And like your mother said, he's an excellent judge of people. Besides, Mark needs a mother and the boy appears to be particularly fond of this woman. He talks about her constantly."

"I certainly hope you aren't marrying her just for Mark's sake," Lucas's mother cautioned him sternly.

"I'm not," he affirmed forcefully.

His mother, Felicity noted, did not look convinced. And neither was she.

"Lucas has always known his own mind," the grandmother spoke up again. She smiled warmly at him. "I'm sure you and your Felicity will make a fine pair."

Well, I'm not, Felicity declared tersely, then slipped back behind her door.

A knock sounded and she peeked out. *But you would like to be,* Lucas said.

Without responding, she closed the door once again. Her gaze scanned her office as she reorientated her mind. To deny his last words would be a lie. All morning she'd been fighting an intense loneliness. Now she was forced to admit it was because she missed him.

Abruptly the memory of the afternoon Jeff had informed her about his pregnant mistress filled her mind. More strongly than ever, the betrayal and humiliation she'd felt that day again swept through her.

The walls of her office seemed suddenly to be closing in on her. She had to get out of there. Working in the garden always helped when she was feeling this way so she headed home.

Thelma was sitting on the porch in her favorite rocking chair, snapping beans, when she arrived. "I'm glad to see you're not going to spend all day behind a desk," her grandmother greeted her with a smile.

"I needed some fresh air," Felicity replied, without even stopping as she continued into the house.

Minutes later she emerged in shorts and sneakers.

"What's wrong?" Thelma demanded worriedly.

"Nothing," she tossed back with schooled nonchalance, stepping off the porch and heading for the toolshed. There she retrieved the hoe. As she began working her way down a row of corn, chopping weeds, emotions she'd long kept suppressed insisted on bubbling to the surface.

"I think you'd better put down that hoe and tell me what's bothering you." Thelma's voice broke into her thoughts.

Felicity glanced over her shoulder to discover her grandmother standing at the edge of the garden, regarding her with an impatient, worried frown.

Again she started to deny that something was bothering her, but instead an acid taste filled her mouth. "At the very least, Jeff could have had the decency to face me and tell me he wanted out of the marriage instead of going behind my back and having an affair," she seethed.

"Well, it's about time you got that out of your system," Thelma said with approval. "I've always thought you were putting too much blame on yourself and being much too civil and rational about his behavior."

Felicity tackled another weed, lifting it with the corner of the hoe then chopping it into little bits. "I treated him fairly, with respect. In return, he made me feel degraded...humiliated."

"That man deserved to have a horsewhip taken to him," Thelma asserted.

Felicity had never cried about her broken marriage. She'd been too proud. Now tears began to flow down her cheeks. But they were not tears of sadness. They were, instead, tears of rage. "He had no right to treat me the way he did!"

"I'm glad to hear you finally giving credit where credit is due," Thelma said with approval.

"He betrayed my trust. He betrayed me!" Felicity growled, the anger she'd been keeping under control for so long spewing forth.

"That's my girl. Get it out before it poisons your system so badly you forget how to trust," Thelma encouraged.

Felicity was suddenly aware of a pounding. It was Lucas. *Go away,* she ordered. Not wanting him to witness her this way, she'd opened the door between them only a crack. Now she closed it securely.

I'm not leaving until I know what's wrong, he returned, his thought so strong it penetrated the sturdy barrier between them.

This is a private catharsis, she insisted.

Jeff Lomax? he asked, irritation evident. *How can you waste tears on that loser?*

Realizing her guard had slipped and the door between them had opened, she flushed with embarrassment. Her first instinct was to slam the barrier shut but pride insisted she correct his misconception first. *I'm not wasting tears on him. I'm just venting a little anger at the way he treated me.*

Sounded like more than just a little.

Felicity was certain she sensed jealousy. A small glow of pleasure eased the humiliation she'd been feeling. *I've been keeping it suppressed too long. It had time to grow.*

"Felicity!"

Felicity's attention jerked back to her grandmother as Thelma's anxious voice interrupted the exchange with Lucas.

"You were acting as if you were a thousand miles away," Thelma continued, studying her with concern.

"That and a few more," Felicity replied, brushing at the now drying streaks of water on her cheeks.

Thelma studied her more closely. "Are you all right?"

Felicity smiled. "I feel better than I have in years."

Thelma's expression relaxed. "I'm glad to hear that."

Now that you have that rat out of your system, don't you think it's time you got on with your life? It was Lucas again.

Yes, she admitted.

With me, he coaxed.

The temptation to surrender to his wishes was close to overwhelming. Sternly she reminded herself of the humiliation learning of Jeff's mistress had caused. *I need time to think,* she returned, visualizing her door and starting to swing it shut. To her surprise, she sensed him smiling.

At least you didn't tell me to get lost, he noted, before the door closed firmly.

Her hand went to her temple where a headache was building.

"I've never known your mind to wander so badly," Thelma said, reminding Felicity of her presence. "All this heavy-duty crying in the afternoon sun could be giving you sunstroke." She took hold of her grand-daughter's arm. "Come up on the porch this minute."

Felicity gave her grandmother no argument.

"Now you sit. I'm going to get you a glass of lem-onade," Thelma instructed when she'd gotten her granddaughter to the porch swing.

Felicity did as she was told. For a moment, her re-solve had seriously weakened and that frightened her. Uncertainty tormented her.

"How do I know when I can trust a man's love to be honest?" she asked when her grandmother returned with the lemonade.

"Use your instincts," Thelma replied, seating her-self in her rocker.

Felicity frowned. "I did that once."

Thelma gave her granddaughter's hand a squeeze. "Then follow your heart."

As her grandmother returned to snapping beans, Fe-licity propped the pillows up on the arm of the swing and laid back. She'd worked hard at not thinking about Jeff Lomax. Now she made herself recall their courtship and their marriage.

She'd married him because he made her feel protected and loved. But she had to admit their physical relationship had lacked a certain passion. He'd treated her more like a china doll than a woman. Being with him had never equaled the sensual pleasure she experienced in those dreams she and Lucas had shared.

Jeff disappeared from her thoughts as Lucas filled her mind. He was a good father and a truly decent man. His image became even clearer, and she recalled the delicious excitement of his kiss. It would be very easy to fall in love with him.

With this realization a fresh doubt assailed her. If she'd fallen in love with Jeff because he made her feel cared for at a time when she was feeling insecure, how could she be certain that the feelings Lucas was stirring within her weren't simply lust brought on by a burst of hormones?

Groaning in frustration, she sat up, then pushed herself to her feet. "I'm going to hoe some more," she announced.

"One thing's for sure," Thelma observed. "We're going to have one of the best-tended gardens in the state."

"I just wish flawed emotions were as easy to spot as weeds," Felicity sighed.

"Uncertainty is a part of life. It's what keeps us from getting bored," Thelma returned.

Felicity frowned. "I wasn't bored before Lucas and Mark walked into my life. I was comfortable."

"You were keeping a large part of yourself locked away. It's time for that part to be freed. It's time for you to let romance back into your life."

Felicity made no response as she picked up the hoe and headed back to the garden. Maybe her grandmother was right. Maybe it was time for her to allow romance back into her life. She just wasn't certain she was prepared for Lucas Carver.

And Felicity certainly wasn't prepared for him to come calling so early, she grumbled the next morning as she splashed water on her face to wake herself and heard him knocking on her door. *Go away. I've got to get ready for church,* she shouted through the barrier.

But as she splashed more water on her face, she suddenly realized how early it was in Seattle and a tremor of fear shot through her. She hadn't sensed any anxiety from him but then with her door in place, she wasn't certain his emotions could travel through. *Wait!* she cried out, quickly drying her face. Raking her hands through her hair to comb it back, she straightened as she opened the door. *Is something wrong? Are you ill? Is Mark ill?*

No. I was just missing you and thought I'd say good morning came his reply. *Wish you were here.*

The empty half of his bed filled her vision. Deep inside embers of desire flamed to life. The thought that being there with him would be enjoyable filled her mind.

You're welcome anytime.

Furious with herself for not guarding her thoughts more carefully, she ordered herself to be more prudent in the future.

You look very appealing early in the morning.

He could see her? Of course he could, she answered her own query as she realized she was looking in a mirror.

I was, however, picturing you in something a little more sexy.

Felicity frowned down at her comfortable, old white cotton nightgown. Thank goodness she'd had something on. *Good day, Mr. Carver,* she retorted and closed the door.

But as she dressed, she couldn't completely erase the memory of his bed. It had looked enticingly inviting.

What she was feeling could easily be merely lust, she told herself as she went downstairs. Determinedly she shoved him to the back of her mind. But later, sitting in church, the loneliness she'd experienced the day before returned with renewed force. Even in the midst of family and friends she was missing Lucas again.

Mentally she groaned. She'd promised herself she would be very, very careful about entering into a romantic entanglement. First there would be friendship and then, once she was certain she could trust the man, she would allow herself to fall in love. Yet, here she was wishing Lucas was sitting beside her. Even more, she realized she felt incomplete without him.

She would not be swept off her feet! she declared fervently. She would behave in a practical and rational manner. After all, she'd barely known the man a week. And even though they did have a rather unique bond, that didn't mean they were a perfect match.

Again she ordered herself to stop thinking about him, and for the rest of the day she did manage to stay busy enough to keep her mind on other things. But at night, lying in bed, the loneliness she was trying to ignore returned to taunt her. Unable to resist, she opened the mental door she'd been keeping securely locked.

There was a flash of activity, then all she could see was a blank wall.

Was he with another woman? she wondered, a sense of betrayal a hundred times worse than that which she'd experienced when she learned of Jeff's mistress flooding over her.

Sorry about shutting you out so abruptly but I'm not used to receiving visitors in my shower.

Felicity's sense of betrayal faded and she became aware of his embarrassment. A mischievous smile played at the corners of her mouth. *I can't believe you're behaving so shyly,* she teased. *Just this morning you were inviting me into your bed.*

This morning I was expecting you. With a playful lecherousness, he added, *But now that I'm over the start you gave me, you're welcome to join me.*

Felicity found herself tempted. She was supposed to be moving slowly, she reminded herself. And she was not supposed to act on her baser instincts, she added curtly. *I'll just be on my way,* she replied, quickly retreating behind her door.

Pulling her covers around her protectively, she moaned in frustration. The man was a definite threat to her resolve. And what if she was right and his attraction toward her was motivated by his desire to please his son? Someday he could find someone who truly pleased him. "I won't make another mistake," she growled.

Chapter Eleven

Felicity was sitting at the kitchen table eating breakfast the next morning when the phone rang.

"If that's Lucas, I've half a mind to hang up on him," Thelma said, irritably. "Maybe you were right about keeping your distance from him. After all the interest he claimed to have in you, I thought he'd have called since he left. But no, there's been nary a word. Clearly he's one of those out-of-sight-out-of-mind kind of men."

Maybe out of sight but never out of mind, Felicity countered mentally. Her fair side refused to allow her grandmother to be angry with Lucas for something he had not done. "I've heard from him," she admitted.

Thelma's anger turned to relief. "I didn't like to think I was that bad a judge of character," she said as she picked up the receiver. After a quick initial greeting, she extended the phone toward Felicity. "It's Zebulon. He wants to speak to you, and he sounds irritated."

Wondering what was bothering him, Felicity took the receiver. "Good morning, Zebulon."

"Don't say as I'd call it that" came his curt response.

A prickling of uneasiness ran along Felicity's spine. "What's wrong?"

"T'ain't nothing wrong. Just that fool Jerome Sayer threatening to make trouble. Got some stupid notion he should get my land once I'm buried. Told him it weren't none of his business what I did with my land." Zebulon's voice became even sterner. "I just wanted to check with you to make certain that will you're drawing up is airtight. Don't want no Sayer getting his hands on my land."

"The will is as airtight as any will can be," she assured him.

"Good," he replied, then added, "I told Sayer I'd have him arrested for trespassing if he ever set foot on my land again."

"Don't worry." Felicity tried to soothe him. "Jerome Sayer can't stop your wishes from being carried out."

"What has Zebulon so worked up?" Thelma asked with concern when Felicity hung up the phone.

"Jerome Sayer has got a real bee in his bonnet about Zebulon's land. He thinks it should be his."

"He was a mean and spiteful child and he grew into a mean and spiteful man. 'Course that seems to run in the Sayer family." Thelma shook her head. "And that wife of his isn't too much better. Both of them are a bit too self-righteous if you ask me. They think they're better than other folk. And they've raised their children to be just as mean-spirited. Except for Emily, of course. I know life was rough for her, but she was lucky to get away from that family when she did."

"I don't think Emily would have turned out like the rest even if she hadn't been cast out by them and left to fend for herself," Felicity replied. "She has a good heart."

Thelma's agreement was cut short by the sound of a vehicle approaching. "Wonder who that could be this early in the morning?"

"I'll see," Felicity said, already heading to the front door. As she stepped out onto the porch a wave of hostility met her.

Remaining in his pickup, Jerome Sayer glared at her. "You better warn that Carver character to stay out of town. We don't need any more strangers moving in around here."

A shiver of fear shook Felicity but she hid it well as she faced the man levelly. "It's a free country, Mr. Sayer. Mr. Carver can live where he chooses."

"Jerome Sayer, you take that inhospitable attitude of yours and get on home," Thelma ordered, coming out to stand beside Felicity.

"I won't be robbed of what is rightfully mine," he growled. Then shifting his truck back into gear, he left a cloud of dust as he took off down the road.

Felicity, are you all right? a groggy voice demanded harshly.

"I'm fine," she replied.

"Of course you are," Thelma said, "Why wouldn't you be? I never raised you to be intimidated by a bully."

Felicity saw her grandmother studying her questioningly and silently groaned. She'd answered Lucas out loud. "And I wasn't," she assured her. "I will admit I'm a little shaken, though. I've never felt such hateful rage," she added, still not ready to tell her grandmother about the unusual connection between her and Lucas.

Lucas was now knocking loudly, refusing to go away. Unable to think with the pounding, she let him in.

Felicity, I want to know what's going on, he demanded. *I felt a jolt of fear from you that was so strong it woke me from a sound sleep.*

I just had a little visit from Jerome Sayer.

"Felicity!" Thelma spoke her name sharply.

She realized her grandmother was again regarding her worriedly.

"Now don't you fret, child," Thelma said when she saw she finally had her granddaughter's attention. "Jerome is a big bully. He'll rant and rave for a while . . . maybe get himself a lawyer, but that'll be the extent of it."

From all she'd heard of Jerome Sayer, Felicity knew her grandmother was probably right. "The man just unnerves me." She gave her shoulders a shake in an attempt to rid herself of the lingering uneasiness left by his visit.

"Come on inside and finish your breakfast," Thelma encouraged gently.

Lucas was still there and Felicity needed some privacy in which to get rid of him. She didn't want to make another slip in front of her grandmother. "I'll join you in a minute," she promised. "The weather's so beautiful this morning, I'd like to stay out here for a moment longer and enjoy it."

"I'll pour you a fresh cup of coffee," Thelma replied, heading back inside.

I wish you wouldn't pop in on me like that, Felicity fumed as soon as she was alone.

You scared me came Lucas's apologetic reply. Then the apology was gone, replaced by angry protectiveness. *If this Sayer person bothers you again, he's going to have to answer to me.*

Fear for Lucas shook her. *I want you to stay away from Jerome Sayer,* she insisted curtly.

I won't go looking for trouble, but I'm not going to stand by and allow him to harass you.

She could feel his arms drawing her into the safe harbor of his embrace and a part of her wanted to enter. Tersely she reminded herself that seeking sanctuary in a man's arms was the mistake she'd made before. Mentally she stepped away from him. *It's you he's got the grievance with. Besides, I don't need a knight in shining armor to come to my rescue. I can take care of myself.*

Suddenly the image of Lucas dressed as a white knight mounted on his sturdy steed filled her mind.

Personally I think I look pretty good in that role, he remarked, letting her know he was the one originating the image.

He did look good...very good, she was forced to agree. Being a knight in shining armor seemed to fit him perfectly. The desire to be his lady fair grew within her. And marrying a woman for his son's sake would certainly be a knightly deed, she reminded herself curtly, determined not to give in to fairy-tale romances. *I've got to go,* she informed him, and before he could respond, she closed the door between them.

"You look like a woman with something serious on her mind," Thelma said when Felicity joined her in the kitchen. "Are you still worried about Jerome?"

"Not really. Like you said, he's a bully. He yells and shouts and threatens and makes people uncomfortable, but that's the extent of his actions." Seating herself at the table, Felicity propped her chin in her hands and studied her grandmother. "How can you tell when love is the lasting kind? Or, maybe even more to the point, how can you tell if what you feel is love and not just lust?"

Thelma's eyes sparkled with interest. "Now, that's certainly a change of subject. Are we talking about Lucas Carver?"

Talking to her grandmother had always helped in the past, Felicity reminded herself, and she did need help. "He's a very good-looking man. It's only natural I'd feel attracted to him. But maybe that attraction is merely physical. Maybe I'm just feeling lonely for male companionship. After all, I'm still a young woman."

Thelma smiled sympathetically. "Is it love or is it lust? That is a dilemma."

"Exactly."

A warm glow of reminiscence came over the older woman's features. "I remember the first time I saw your grandfather. My family had just moved here to the valley. I was ten and he was fourteen. He was walking down the road with a fishing pole. I thought he was the cutest boy I'd ever seen. From that moment on, he was the only man who could hold my attention."

Felicity frowned. "I wasn't so lucky at spotting my Mr. Right at first glance."

"True," Thelma conceded. A momentary silence fell between them, then she asked, "Was your reaction when you first met Lucas the same as when you first met Jeff?"

Felicity forced herself to recall the first time she'd seen Jeff Lomax. "No, the reaction wasn't the same," she confessed. "But then I wasn't the same person in each case. When I first met Jeff, I was immature, unsure of myself. His attention was flattering and he seemed to offer a secure sanctuary. I'm more mature now. I don't feel the need to have a man to lean on.''

"So how did you feel when you first saw Lucas?" Thelma asked.

"There was a strong physical attraction," Felicity confessed. "Very strong," she added, recalling the dreams that had quickly followed. She frowned in frustration. "But that just brings me back to my first question…how do I tell the difference between love and lust." Her frown deepened. "And then there's the question of his feelings for me. He claims to love me and my instincts tell me that he's being truthful. But then my instincts told me that Jeff was being truthful, too, and he was, but it was a conditional truth. How can I be certain Lucas hasn't convinced himself, for his son's sake, that what is merely a strong lust is really love? If that's the case, then after a while, he'll want out of the marriage.''

For a long moment Thelma was silent, then she said, "I suppose you're just going to have to ask yourself if Lucas is worth taking a chance on."

"So that's the solution? I'm supposed to throw caution to the wind and simply take a chance?" Felicity shook her head.

But a few minutes later as she drove toward town, Felicity found herself again considering Lucas's good points. She knew from watching him with his son that he was a good father. He also appeared to have an honest relationship with his family. Clearly they did not all agree with each other but there was love between them that she sensed easily. And he certainly aroused her passion.

It's the bad points that count, she reminded herself, and began listing those. He was stubbornly persistent. But that wasn't always a mark against a person, she found herself arguing. She tried to think of something that would clearly make him an undesirable choice. Nothing came to mind. She hadn't known him long enough to discover his annoying traits, she reasoned.

Reaching her office, she ordered herself to put the man out of her mind and concentrate on business.

And she was successful for the first few hours. But when Peggy had left to have lunch with her husband, and Felicity settled back in her chair to eat the sandwich she'd brought, Lucas Carver again filled her thoughts. Even when he was over a thousand miles away he was a nuisance, she fumed.

A sudden inspiration struck her. To let him know she was there, she knocked on the mental door she'd erected between them, then opened it. He was seated at a desk cluttered with files and papers. *I was just getting some paperwork organized in preparation for my replacement to take over,* he informed her. *You're a very pleasant interruption.*

Maybe not, she warned.

And why not?

I've been wondering about your faults, she replied bluntly.

What about them?

She sensed a hint of defensiveness coming from him. *I was wondering what they are. Everyone has them. I'm willing to exchange one for one with you.*

Amusement replaced his defensiveness. *You do have a no-nonsense way of getting to know a person.*

A fit of nervousness caused her to consider backing out. Her jaw firmed with determination. She'd come this far, she was going through with this. If she didn't, she'd spend the afternoon wondering about him and not getting anything constructive done. *In the morning, I'm generally not good company until I've had my first cup of coffee,* she confessed.

Guess I'll have to start bringing you coffee in bed once we're married, he returned with a sultry flavor.

This subtle promise of early-morning trysts made Felicity's toes wanted to curl with delight. That's strictly lust, she admonished herself. *It's your turn to confess to a fault,* she reminded him.

I like to read the newspaper at the breakfast table.

Felicity experienced a territorial urge. *Do you do the cryptogram and the crossword?*

No, I pretty much concentrate on the financial and editorial pages followed by sports and the comics.

Felicity breathed a mental sigh of relief. *Good, because I like to do the puzzles. They wake up my brain.*

We sound highly compatible to me, he observed.

As if he were there, Felicity could feel herself being drawn into his embrace. The urge to go into his arms and test their compatibility was strong. Determined to keep her mind on the course she'd set for this encounter, she mentally stepped back out of his reach. Recalling a habit of hers that had gotten on Jeff's nerves, she said, *I tap my fingernails when I'm upset or trying to work out a difficult problem.*

I pace, Lucas confessed, respecting her wishes and keeping his distance. *I'm also a workaholic. Since Mark came into my life, I've made an effort to spend more time at home, but I still work long hours.* A playfully lecherous quality entered his thoughts. *However, I promise I won't neglect you.*

Felicity's blood heated. She frowned at herself and again ordered herself to stick to business. *How can you be so certain what you feel for me isn't just because you want Mark to have the mother he wants so he won't feel neglected?*

She is currently on vacation so you have not seen her, but Mark has a full-time nanny.

The image of a motherly looking woman in her early forties filled Felicity's mind.

Jane dotes on him as does his grandmother, great-grandmother and grandfather. I can assure you he does not feel neglected, Lucas stated.

Maybe you're afraid he'll stop speaking if you don't marry me, she challenged, determined to get all of her doubts out in the open.

He's been talking a blue streak ever since we got home. I'm certain that, like you, he won't return to being mute. Again he began drawing her into his embrace. *I want you for myself, Felicity,* he assured her huskily.

The urge to believe him was close to overwhelming. *This is all happening too fast.* Quickly she moved away from him and across the threshold of her door. *I need time to think,* she told him and began to close the door.

He placed a hand on the barrier. *And I think we need to have this conversation face-to-face rather than mind to mind. I'll be back in Smytheshire tomorrow.* Then releasing his hold on the door, he allowed her to close it.

Felicity sat staring absently, barely cognizant of her surroundings. All she could think about was that Lucas would be there in the flesh the next day. Excitement raced through her at the thought of actually seeing him. Don't act rashly, she ordered herself.

A year should be sufficient, she decided. She would give herself a year to get to know him and determine if they could have a life together. Twelve months suddenly seemed like an interminable amount of time. Six months might be enough, she conceded. A scowl spread over her face. She was beginning to sound like a teenager in heat.

Issuing a low growl of frustration, she forced her mind back to the papers in front of her.

But for the rest of the day, the temptation to again seek out Lucas taunted her. By the time dinner was over, she was exhausted from the struggle to keep a distance between them. Going out onto the porch, she curled up in the swing and stared up at the starlit sky. He'd decided too quickly that he wanted to marry her, she insisted to herself. Pleasing Mark had to be at least part of his motivation.

She thought back to their first encounter. From the beginning, she'd sensed a lustful interest on his part. "Lustful" was the key word, her practical side interjected. Mix a little—make that a lot—of lust with wanting to make his son happy and Lucas could easily have convinced himself he was in love with her.

She breathed a tired sigh. Uncertainty plagued her. But there was one thing of which she was now sure. She wanted a husband and family. Since her divorce, she'd worked hard to convince herself she was happy on her own. Now she was forced to admit that was a lie. Her bed felt lonely and there was an emptiness in her life she could no longer ignore.

But how could she avoid another mistake? Her head began to throb. Time will tell, she assured herself. The problem was that she wanted Lucas's arms around her right that minute. He does inspire lusty thoughts, she mused and went inside to bed.

Chapter Twelve

Felicity awoke the next morning with a sense of excited expectation. She was behaving like a teenager who knew she was going to see the object of her latest crush, she admonished herself. Still, the excitement lingered.

On the way to work she had to fight the urge to seek him out. For the umpteenth time she warned herself that she could get badly hurt if she didn't behave prudently. Slow and careful were to be her watchwords. And, above all, she would guard her heart.

But when he hadn't made his presence known by midafternoon, her patience began to wear thin. Maybe he'd had second thoughts. Deep inside she experienced a sharp jab of pain. "At least I was smart enough to behave with caution," she congratulated herself. But she didn't feel like cheering.

Suddenly she knew he was nearby. Glancing out the window, she saw him coming up her walk. Shoving her chair back, she rose and was halfway to her office door before she realized what she was doing. Abruptly she stopped herself. Running into his arms was definitely not behaving with caution and reserve. And she had vowed she would practice both.

A knock sounded on her office door. Quickly she turned and grabbed a paper off her desk to make it appear as if she were busy and had not noticed his approach. "Come in."

"Peggy said you had a few free minutes," he said, entering and closing the door behind him.

Just seeing him brought a surge of joy. "Did you have a good flight?" she asked.

An impatience flickered in his eyes. "Knowing I'd be seeing you today was all I could think about," he replied, continuing toward her.

She knew he was going to take her in his arms and ordered herself to hurriedly put her desk between her and him. But her legs refused to obey.

"You look delicious." Capturing her face in his hands, he kissed her. "And you definitely taste and feel much better in person," he added gruffly.

"So do you," she heard herself admitting.

"Wait, you can't just burst in there!" Peggy's voice penetrated the air.

Abruptly releasing Felicity, Lucas turned to the office door just as it was thrust open.

Seeing Jerome Sayer and his son, Patrick, Felicity stiffened for battle.

"I tried to stop them," Peggy was saying angrily from behind the men.

Ignoring both Peggy and Felicity, Jerome's full attention focused on Lucas. "I thought that was you in that rental car," he growled. "You're Lucas Carver, aren't you?"

"Yes," Lucas replied, with cool calm.

Dislike glistened in the big farmer's eyes. "I'm Jerome Sayer, and I've got some business with you."

Lucas regarded him levelly. "I guessed who you were."

The sneer on Jerome's face deepened and Felicity realized that Lucas's self-assured manner was causing the farmer's rage to grow stronger. Clearly Jerome had planned on intimidating Lucas and his plan wasn't working.

Lucas took a step forward, placing himself squarely between Felicity and Jerome. "And what business do we have to discuss?"

Staring at Lucas's back, Felicity had never felt the kind of protection she sensed right now. There was a strong, unbendable strength about him that Jeff had never had. But that didn't mean he couldn't get hurt if Jerome became violent. Stepping out from behind Lucas, she said curtly, "Mr. Sayer, you have no right to burst into my office. If you do not leave immediately, I'll call Chief Brant."

"I've come to say my piece, and I intend to say it," Jerome snarled. He glared at Lucas. "You'd better not be trying to steal my birthright."

"I've got no interest in any birthright of yours," Lucas assured the man, again stepping between him and Felicity.

"Zebulon's land is my birthright."

"I think he might disagree with you on that point."

Jerome issued a snort of disgust. "You're not welcome here."

Felicity again stepped out from behind Lucas. "It's you who is not welcome here," she told Jerome. Looking past him, she said, "Call Chief Brant, Peggy."

As Peggy lifted the receiver, Patrick laid a hand on his father's arm. "I think we should leave."

"You should listen to your son," Felicity advised.

Jerome glared at Lucas for a moment longer. "If Zebulon tries to leave his land to you, I'll see you in court." Then jerking free from his son's hold, he strode out.

"This isn't the way I envisioned my return," Lucas said as the front door slammed behind the two men.

"I'll try to see that you aren't disturbed again," Peggy promised, returning the receiver to its cradle, the call to the chief unmade.

Giving Peggy a nod of thanks, Lucas closed the door of Felicity's office. Then turning to her, he grinned. "You'd fit well into a suit of armor yourself. I liked having you by my side. We make a good team."

Felicity found herself thinking the same thing. Cautioning herself to proceed with caution, she took a step back, placing more distance between them. "Where's Mark?" she asked, noticing the boy wasn't there and realizing how much she'd missed him as well.

"I left him in Seattle to be spoilt by his grandparents," Lucas replied. "I wanted some time alone with you."

Felicity knew that time alone with him could be very dangerous to her resolve. On the other hand, being with him was the only way she could learn if his feelings ran as deeply as he claimed. The fear of making another mistake again swept through her and she pictured Lucas leaving her for another woman. Her stomach knotted in pain.

"Felicity, what's wrong?" he demanded.

"Nothing playing it safe won't prevent," she replied.

He frowned and she knew he'd guessed what was on her mind. "You are safe with me," he assured her.

She wanted to believe him but her fear remained strong. Needing some time alone, she glanced at her watch. "My next appointment should be arriving any minute now."

His gaze leveled on her. "I'm going to go by and see Zebulon. I'll pick you up at your place at six for dinner." Without giving her a chance to respond, he left.

Rounding her desk, Felicity sank into her chair. Closing her eyes, she rested her face in her hands. Falling in love with Lucas would be very easy. Again she envisioned him leaving her for another woman and again the pain was so intense she felt nauseous. "If I take my time and don't rush into anything, I'll be safe," she assured herself. Still, the fear lingered.

Her intercom buzzed announcing the arrival of her next client and she ordered herself to concentrate on her work. She was succeeding when a jolt of surprise so powerful it penetrated the mental barrier she was keeping between herself and Lucas startled her. It was followed by a rush of fear. Something had Lucas terrified!

She jerked open the door. Her view was through the windshield of a car and Suicide Curve was just ahead. This piece of road had been given that name by the locals because the curve was unusually sharp with a fifty-foot drop on one side and a solid rock face on the other. To take it at more than twenty miles an hour could land a person in the hospital or the cemetery.

At the moment Lucas was careening toward it. Through his eyes, she saw the front end of a truck in the rearview mirror. Lucas was on the precipice side of the road. When he reached the curve, at this speed, he would go over the side.

Mentally she gripped the wheel with him. He turned sharply toward the cliff. The momentum spun the car. The air bag burst out of the steering wheel to protect him from going forward. His head banged against the side window, then the force was sending him in the opposite direction. His seat belt kept him from being tossed into the passenger's seat as that side of the car careened against the cliff. The scene in front of her eyes went black.

Felicity's vocal cords were frozen with fear. The thought that he might have been killed brought a terror so intense she couldn't breath. Mentally she screamed his name.

For what was the longest moment of her life, there was only silence, then she again was seeing the air bag. Her head began to swim from lack of oxygen and she gasped for breath.

I'm shaken but I'm fine, he assured her.

"Felicity! Shall I call Peggy? You're as pale as a ghost. Are you going to faint?" an anxious female voice broke through to Felicity's consciousness.

She blinked her own eyes back into focus to discover Leona Boggs already on her feet and heading around the desk to aid her. "I suddenly don't feel so well," she said shakily. "It must have been something I ate for lunch."

Leona nodded knowingly. "Probably one of those fancy food additives. Might as well just eat the cardboard box some of these new processed foods come in."

"Could we finish this another day?" Felicity asked, already out of her chair and heading to the sanctity of her private bathroom.

"Yes, of course," Leona called out to her departing back.

Standing with her back against the closed door, Felicity closed her eyes and focused again on Lucas. He was opening the door of his car and getting out. On the opposite side of the road, where the curve began, were black skid marks and a break in the low metal barrier.

Satisfied Lucas was dazed and shaken but all right, Felicity's panic subsided enough for her to think more clearly. *I'm going to call the chief,* she informed him, leaving her bathroom only to discover Peggy waiting just beyond the door. She couldn't make the call in front of her secretary. How in the world would she explain how she knew about the accident?

"You look terrible. I'll call Dr. Prescott," Peggy said, starting to pick up the phone.

"No," Felicity returned sharply. That was too sharp, she admonished herself and forced her voice into a calmer mode. "No, really, I'll be fine. But I need to leave. Cancel the rest of my appointments. I just need to make a quick call and then I'm going home." Mentally she breathed a sigh of relief. At least the accident had happened on her route home so she wouldn't have to explain how she'd just happened onto the scene.

Peggy continued to linger. "Are you sure you'll be fine on your own? Maybe I should drive you."

"I'm sure." Felicity made a shooing motion with her hands in an attempt to get the secretary out of her office. "The call I have to make is private, and I want to get it over with so I can leave."

"Well, your color is coming back," Peggy conceded, backing toward the door, then finally exiting.

Grabbing the receiver, Felicity dialed the police station. "There's been an accident at Suicide Curve on Hollow Road. They'll need an ambulance," she said as soon as the dispatcher answered.

"That's that sharp curve about eight miles west of town on Hollow Road?" the dispatcher verified.

"Right," Felicity replied.

"I'll need your name," the woman requested.

"Just send help," Felicity returned and hung up.

"That was fast," Peggy observed as Felicity hurried out of her office.

"I just want to get home," Felicity explained, practically jogging toward the door.

"Drive carefully," Peggy called after her.

Slipping into the driver's seat of her car, Felicity again turned her mind to Lucas. He was on his way down the steep rocky terrain of the precipice. Below she saw an overturned pickup truck, its wheels still spinning. She recognized the truck. *Jerome Sayer.* She flashed the name at him.

He gave her a mental nod and his gaze scanned to the body of a man lying on the ground a few feet from the vehicle.

From the clothes, I'd guess that was Patrick, she told him.

Again he gave a mental nod of agreement. A sudden jolt of renewed fear emitting from him shook her and she realized he was sliding. *Be careful,* she shrieked.

I am, he returned, regaining control and returning his full attention to his descent.

Forcing the scene of the accident out of her mind, she started her engine and pulled out onto the road. It took willpower to concentrate on her driving and not flash back to Lucas. She had to keep reminding herself that she didn't want to be in an accident while trying to get to him. After what seemed like an interminable drive, she knew she was nearing the curve. Ahead she saw the flashing lights of a police car.

Half-crushed against the side of the cliff, was Lucas's rental car. The realization of how close he'd come to being killed caused bile to rise in her throat. Pulling off onto a widened section of shoulder just below the curve, she left her car and hurried to the scene.

Flares had been set to warn approaching motorists of the accident and Thatcher Brant was on his way down the steep slope. Below she could see the flipped-over truck. Her gaze shifted to the man lying a few feet away. Lucas was kneeling beside him.

Standing at the broken guardrail, she closed her eyes and joined her mind to Lucas's.

"You're going to be all right," he was assuring the injured man.

Felicity had guessed correctly. It was Patrick.

Thatcher reached the bottom of the ravine and Lucas's gaze swung to him. "Jerome's still in the truck," he shouted to the chief. "I couldn't get him out. I think he's dead."

Thatcher took a quick look in the cab, then joined Lucas. "It's my guess he was killed instantly," the chief said. His gaze shifted to Patrick. "Don't know how you managed to survive in that cab. It's pretty well crushed."

"I was thrown clear," Patrick replied, wincing from pain.

"He's got a broken leg and arm, most likely some internal injuries and a nasty bump on his head," Lucas said.

Thatcher's tone became official. "What happened?"

"I was on my way to visit Zebulon," Lucas replied. "Suddenly that pickup came up behind me and tried to push me into this ravine. I managed to turn my wheels and ended up against the cliff. The truck went over the edge."

"I don't know what came over Pa. He's got a temper and lately he's been getting meaner, but he's never done anything this crazy," Patrick said, his voice dazed as if he was still having a hard time believing the accident had occurred.

Thatcher turned his attention to the injured man. "I think you'd better tell me what this is all about."

"We were following Carver. Pa had decided to wait outside that Burrow woman's office and talk to him. But he wanted it private and she'd threatened to call you so we were going to follow him and talk to him where she wouldn't be sticking her nose in. When he headed out of town, at first Pa was glad. 'We'll have some real privacy now,' he told me. Then Carver turned onto Hollow Road and Pa realized he was heading for Zebulon's place. 'Going to take a look at what is rightfully mine and probably gloat a bit, too,' Pa said."

Patrick tried to shift and winced with pain.

"Go on," Thatcher coaxed.

"Well, Pa's temper got worse the further we came down Hollow Road. He got to muttering about what was rightfully his. Then suddenly, he was speeding up and the next thing I knew he'd bumped into Carver's car and was pushing it toward the drop-off. I yelled at him to stop, but he refused to listen. Next thing I knew, the car was gone and we were going over the edge. My door popped open, and I went flying. That's all I remember until I came to and saw Carver leaning over me."

"It was your Pa's mean-spiritedness that killed him," Thatcher said grimly. "I hope you take a lesson from this."

Patrick merely groaned and closed his eyes.

A siren in the background caught Felicity's attention and she glanced over her shoulder to see the ambulance approaching.

It took awhile for the rescue workers to get Patrick into the metal basket and then up to the ambulance. As for Lucas, other than a few cuts and bruises, they couldn't find anything wrong with him and he refused to be taken to the hospital in Greenfield. Felicity, however, insisted on taking him back into Smytheshire to see Dr. Prescott.

After X-raying him and checking him over thoroughly, Reid Prescott determined that Lucas would be sore but had no serious injuries.

In spite of the doctor's assurance, Felicity continued to remain anxious. "I'm taking you home with me. I don't think you should be left on your own," she said as she and Lucas left the doctor's office and climbed back into her car. "I want to keep an eye on you and make certain Dr. Prescott didn't miss anything."

He grinned rakishly. "I like the sound of that."

And so did she, she admitted, making a quick stop at Betty Truesdale's to pick up his suitcase and personal belongings.

Turning onto Hollow Road, the panic she'd experienced when the accident occurred again swept through her. It had been more than panic, she confessed. If he had died a part of her would have died as well. The debate she'd been having with herself for the past couple of hours ended. "I've decided to marry you," she said stiffly.

He grinned. "Can I assume that the thought of nearly losing me caused you to admit to yourself that you do love me?"

Although she could no longer resist the thought of marrying him, she was still uncertain of his true motives. Pride coupled with the fear of being hurt refused to allow her to admit even to herself that what she felt for him was really love. "You've made me realize that I want a family and you are the logical choice. I'm strongly attracted to you. Besides, being married to someone else and having you popping in and out of my mind could prove to be not only disconcerting but embarrassing. And I am extremely fond of Mark."

When he made no response, she glanced at him out of the corner of her eye. He was scowling at the road ahead and she sensed a strong feeling of withdrawal. Clearly, now that she'd agreed to what he wanted, he was having second thoughts!

Attempting to ignore the pain of rejection twisting her stomach, she congratulated herself for not opening up her heart to him. Still, hot tears burned behind her eyes. Slamming on the brakes, she pulled over onto the shoulder, then turned to regard him cynically. "I was right all along. You were only interested in me for Mark's sake. My capitulation has caused you to face reality and you realize you don't really want to marry me. Well, consider yourself freed!"

She started to pull back onto the road, but he caught her wrist and pressed on the brake. "What I want is for you to be madly, passionately in love me," he growled.

"I don't want to be in love. I'm not ready to take that chance yet," she confessed tightly.

"Then take me to Betty's or Zebulon's place," he ordered, releasing her.

"We're nearer to Zebulon's place, and he'll keep a close eye on you," she said stiffly.

Pulling back onto the road, she could feel his anger. The loneliness that had taunted her when he was in Seattle now came back, only this time it was deeper and darker and much more intense. She frowned at the road ahead. "From the day you arrived in town, you've turned my world upside down. I was restless all that day. I predicted a huge storm coming. Instead you drove down our road and into my life. All I ever wanted was a quiet, peaceful existence."

"You'll discover that living the life of a little mouse all hidden away from your emotions down in your little cozy mouse hole can get very lonely," he cautioned curtly.

"Mice never get lonely. They breed too easily," she returned, without thinking. Suddenly the image of being in his arms in his bed filled her mind. She shoved it out. That was merely lust, she told herself.

But as she rounded Suicide Curve the panic she'd experienced when she'd thought he'd been injured or maybe even killed flooded through her. She recalled the sensation of a void so dark and deep there had not seemed to be any bottom to it. No longer could she deny the truth to herself or to him. They were on a straight stretch of road now, but she did not look at him as she said tightly, "I do."

She could feel his guardedness like a physical shield as he glanced toward her. "You do what?"

"I love you madly...passionately," she confessed.

"Pull over," he ordered sternly.

She sensed his guard still in place. This was not the reaction she'd anticipated. Had she been right all along? Now that he had won completely, was he so eager to get away from her that he preferred to walk the rest of the way to Zebulon's? The temptation to reach out and touch his mind was strong but she had no desire to face his rejection that closely.

When she had pulled over and shifted into Park, he turned off the ignition. Then getting out, he rounded the car and opened her door. "You say you love me, but all I sense from you is restraint. Step out here and kiss me."

He was right, she admitted. Her fear of making a mistake was still strong and causing her to hold back. Nervously she climbed out of the car.

"This won't hurt a bit," he assured her.

As his arms circled her and his lips found hers, a feeling of oneness pervaded every fiber of her being. A warmth like none she'd ever experienced before flowed through her. Her fears and doubts no longer mattered. She knew this was where she belonged.

* * * * *

COMING NEXT MONTH

#1132 SHEIK DADDY—Barbara McMahon
Super Fabulous Fathers

Years ago, Sheik "Ben" Shalik had loved Megan O'Sullivan with his whole heart. Now he was back, ready to sweep her off her feet. But could he forgive Megan for keeping their daughter a secret?

#1133 MAIL ORDER WIFE—Phyllis Halldorson
Valentine Brides

Mail order bride Coralie Dixon expected anything from her husband-to-be, except outright rejection! Handsome bachelor Jim Buckley *said* he wasn't interested, but his actions spoke differently....

#1134 CINDERELLA BRIDE—Christine Scott
Valentine Brides

Tall, dark and stirringly handsome, Ryan Kendrick was a perfect Prince Charming. But his "convenient" wedding proposal was hardly the fairy-tale marriage Cynthia Gilbert had been hoping for!

#1135 THE HUSBAND HUNT—Linda Lewis
Valentine Brides

Sarah Brannan was all set to say "I do." But then Jake Logan asked her to *live* with him—not marry him. So Sarah set out to turn the reluctant Jake into her willing groom.

#1136 MAKE-BELIEVE MOM—Elizabeth Sites
Valentine Brides

Prim and proper Laura Gardiner was shocked by rancher Nick Rafland's scandalous proposal. Nick needed a make-believe mom for his little nieces, not a real wife. But Laura wanted to be a true-blue bride....

#1137 GOING TO THE CHAPEL—Alice Sharpe
Valentine Brides

Elinor Bosley ran a wedding chapel, though she'd vowed never to walk down its aisle. Then she met sexy Tom Rex and his adorable four-year-old son. And Elinor started hearing wedding bells of her own!

They're the hardest working, sexiest women in the Lone Star State...they're

Daughters OF TEXAS

Annette Broadrick

The O'Brien sisters: Megan, Mollie and Maribeth. Meet them and the men who want to capture their hearts in these titles from Annette Broadrick:

MEGAN'S MARRIAGE
(February, Silhouette Desire #979)
The *MAN OF THE MONTH* is getting married to *very* reluctant bride Megan O'Brien!

INSTANT MOMMY
(March, Silhouette Romance #1139)
A *BUNDLE OF JOY* brings Mollie O'Brien together with the man she's always loved.

THE GROOM, I PRESUME?
(April, Silhouette Desire #992)
Maribeth O'Brien's been left at the altar—but this bride won't have to wait long for wedding bells to ring!

Don't miss the DAUGHTERS OF TEXAS—three brides waiting to lasso the hearts of their very own cowboys! Only from

Bestselling author

RACHEL LEE

takes her Conard County series to new heights with

A CONARD COUNTY Reckoning

This March, Rachel Lee brings readers a brand-new, longer-length, out-of-series title featuring the characters from her successful Conard County miniseries.

Janet Tate and Abel Pierce have both been betrayed and carry deep, bitter memories. Brought together by great passion, they must learn to trust again.

"Conard County is a wonderful place to visit! Rachel Lee has crafted warm, enchanting stories. These are wonderful books to curl up with and read. I highly recommend them."
—*New York Times* bestselling author
Heather Graham Pozzessere

Available in March, wherever Silhouette books are sold.

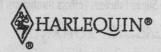

Coming this February from

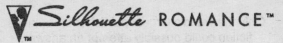 Silhouette ROMANCE™

Expanding upon our ever-popular Fabulous Fathers program, these larger than-life dads are going *even farther* beyond daddy duty—to protect their children at any cost—and gain the love of unforgettable women!

Don't miss the debut of Super-Fabulous Fathers:

SHEIK DADDY
by Barbara McMahon

Sheik Ben Shalik was determined to make things right with Megan O'Sullivan—the one woman who'd haunted his dreams—and with the daughter he'd never known existed. Though Megan swore it was over, he'd be damned if he'd allow fate to take away his family...again!

Looking for more Super-Fabulous Fathers throughout the year... only in Silhouette ROMANCE™